HOLD UP
THE SKY

JANE LOUISE CURRY

HOLD UP THE SKY

and OTHER NATIVE AMERICAN TALES *from* TEXAS *and the* SOUTHERN PLAINS

Illustrated

by

JAMES WATTS

MARGARET K. McELDERRY BOOKS
New York London Toronto Sydney Singapore

Margaret K. McElderry Books
An imprint of Simon & Schuster Children's Publishing Division
1230 Avenue of the Americas,
New York, New York 10020

The text for this book is set in Guardi Roman.
The illustrations for this book are rendered in pencil.

Printed in the United States of America
2 4 6 8 10 9 7 5 3 1
Library of Congress Cataloging-in-Publication Data
Curry, Jane Louise.
Hold up the sky : and other Native American tales from Texas and the Southern Plains / Jane Louise Curry ; illustrated by James Watts.—1st ed.
p. cm.
Summary: Retells twenty-six tales from Native Americans whose traditional lands were in Texas and the Southern Plains, and provides a brief introduction to the history of each tribe.
Includes bibliographical references.
ISBN 0-689-85287-8
I. Indians of North America—Texas—Folklore. 2. Indians of North America—Great Plains—Folklore. 3. Tales—Texas. 4. Tales—Great Plains. [1. Indians of North America—Texas—Folklore. 2. Indians of North America—Great Plains—Folklore. 3. Folklore—Texas. 4. Folklore—Great Plains.] I. Watts, James, 1955- ill. II. Title.
E78.T4 C88 2003
398.2'089'970764—dc21
2002016519

FIRST
EDITION

For David, Judy, Suzanne—and Myra and Sandy
—J. L. C.

To the Big Sky guys
—J. W.

Contents

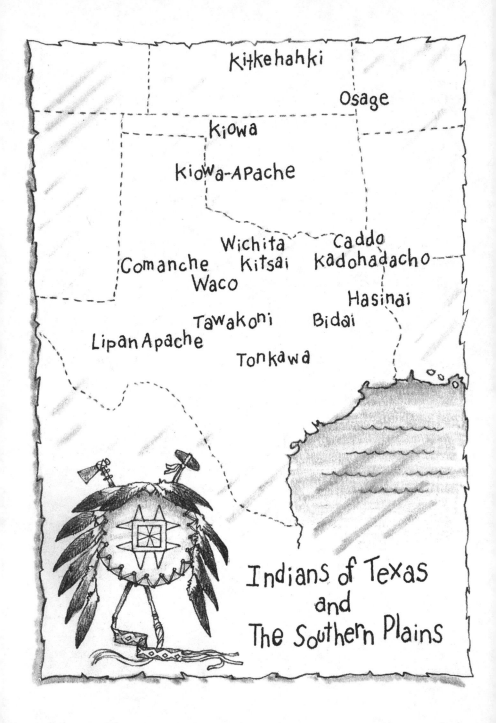

Kitkehahki

Osage

Kiowa

Kiowa-Apache

Wichita
Comanche   Kitsai   Caddo
Waco   Kadohadacho

Hasinai
Tawakoni   Bidai
Lipan Apache
Tonkawa

Indians of Texas
and
The Southern Plains

ABOUT THE TRIBES OF TEXAS
AND THE SOUTHERN PLAINS

From the Avavares, Arbadao, and other fisher-hunter-gatherers of the Texas coast who vanished after the sixteenth century to the remnant of the later Karankawa that was wiped out in 1858, the early peoples of that coast all have disappeared, leaving behind little but their names. The inland Bidai and other tribes in eastern Texas are gone too, leaving no tales behind them because the invading European colonists and Texan settlers did not listen to them. Of the early Texas tribes only the Tonkawan- and Caddoan-speaking farmers of central and eastern Texas survived to tell their tales to scholars and collectors of folklore.

Much changed with the coming of horses, brought to America by the Spanish. With horses Indian hunters could follow the buffalo herds, and so the farming tribes gained new neighbors. Comanche, Kiowan, Lipan Apache, and Kiowa-Apache hunters from the west and north moved into the Southern Plains to become nomads, following the buffalo. From the east came the Siouan Osage and Quapaw, crowded out of their own lands east of the Mississippi.

The tribes of Texas and the Southern Plains have left us a feast of stories from at least five different language "families" (related tribes that spoke similar languages) and five distinct cultures. Some were told to teach caution to children, some to mock folly and self-importance, and others to stir fear or wonder or laughter in every heart around the campfire. The world of the tales is a world as much of magical animals, who are also people, and humans who can choose to become animals, as it is of everyday birds and beasts and men and women.

Step into the story circle and listen. . . .

HOLD UP
THE SKY

THE BEGINNING OF THE WORLD

Tejas (Hasinai)

Ayo-Caddi-Aymay, as the Tejas people called God, was the one and only God, and whatever he did turned out for the best. But, said the Tejas, he had help. At the beginning of the First Time, when there was only earth and darkness, Old Man appeared. In his hand he held an acorn, and the acorn opened and grew—not into an oak tree, but into a magical woman. Old Man wished to make a heaven, and so together he and Acorn Woman put in place a great circle of timber to hold up the sky. The timber circle was so wide that if you looked off toward the west, the dry mountains hid it. To the north, the grass of the rolling prairie hid it. To the south, the far edge of the sea hid it, and to the east it was hidden by the green hills. When the work was finished, Acorn Woman climbed up into the heavens, where every day she still gives new birth to the sun and moon, to rain, frost, and snow, to lightning and thunder, and to the corn.

In the world under the new sky there lived only

one woman, and in time she had two daughters. One day when the sisters were out by themselves gathering food, a huge and terrible monster charged out of the bushes, straight at them. *"Caddaja!"* the girls cried as they turned and ran. "A devil! A demon!" Its red eyes blazed like hot coals, and its horns were so wide that their tips stretched out of sight.

One girl was not quick enough. The *caddaja* snatched at her, caught her in its claws, gobbled her up, swallowed her down, and looked around for her sister. Her sister had run on until she came to a very tall pine tree. Its faraway top seemed the safest place to hide. She climbed up to the very tip of the topmost branch, but the giant *caddaja* sniffed out her path. It lifted up its ugly head and spied the shadow of her shape through the pine boughs.

It tried to climb the tree, but fell back. It tried again and fell back again, for it was too heavy for climbing.

It tried with its sharp claws and strong horns to cut down the tree or break it. The tree was strong, but it groaned and whipped back and forth. The girl knew as she clung fast to her branch that the tree could not hold out for long. She looked down.

Below, on one side of the tree, the monster

rammed the tree trunk and roared. At the foot of the tree on the other side lay a small pond. The girl knew its waters, black and deep. Quickly she unwrapped her legs from the branch, dangled for a moment, held her breath, and dropped straight down. Down, down through the water she went, like an arrow. The angry *caddaja* ran around the tree and bent to suck up the water. As he sucked, he spewed it away so that he could scoop her up from the bottom. But he did not find her.

She had fooled him. Below ground, a hidden stream fed the pond, and the girl swam along it. She came up far away, where the stream flowed out into the sunshine, and ran home to tell her mother all that had happened. Afterward, she and her mother returned to the place where the sister had died. There, caught in an acorn cup, they found a single drop of blood. They covered it with another acorn cup, and the mother placed it safely in her bosom for the journey home. Once there, she put it in a pottery jar, covered the mouth of the jar, and set it in a corner.

In the night, the mother heard a scratching sound that seemed to come from the jar. She went to look. When she uncovered the jar, she discovered that the drop of blood had grown into a little boy no bigger than her little finger. Startled, she replaced the cover on the jar. The next night she and her daughter heard the same noise. When they sat up in alarm, they saw the jar break, and a full-grown young man step out.

"Grandson!" the mother cried out in joy, and embraced him. "Oh, welcome, son of my daughter!"

The young man looked around. "Where is my mother?"

His grandmother and aunt told him of the terrible *caddaja,* of his mother's death, and of the blood drop in the acorn cup.

"I will find it! I will find that giant demon and kill it!" the Blood-Drop Boy cried out.

So his grandmother made him a bow and an arrow, and the next morning he set out. When at last he found the giant monster, he raised his bow and shot his arrow so deep into it that the monster fled, and was never seen again.

Yet that *caddaja* was only one of the many that hated all human beings and caused great terror among the first people. When Blood-Drop Boy returned home, his grandmother and aunt told him that a world full of *caddajas* was so frightening that they wished to leave it. The rest of the men and women and children who had appeared on earth after Grandmother were turning themselves into animal people—bears, otters, dogs, deer, coyotes—to escape the hatred of the monsters.

"It is not yet a good world for humans,"

Grandmother said. "Perhaps one day it will be. But for us, let us go up to *Cachao-ayo,* the sky above, and watch over the earth from there."

So Blood-Drop Boy went up into the heavens with them, and for all the days and years that followed watched over and guided the world below.

COYOTE MAKES THE SUN

Kiowa-Apache

In the very first days of the First Days, the earth and the sky were dark. Coyote had heard that many animal people lived nearby in the darkness, and he went looking for them. One by one, he found Black Hawk and Jackrabbit, Prairie Chicken and Turtle.

To each he said, "You are just the one I need. You must come to a council tonight to see what we can do about this darkness and the cold."

At the council that night, Black Hawk, Jackrabbit, Prairie Chicken, and Turtle sat in a circle and shivered while Coyote explained why he had brought them together. "This cold and this darkness have lasted long enough," he began.

"Hoh, yes!" squawked Prairie Chicken. "And we are just the ones to put an end to it."

"Hai! We are!" shrieked Black Hawk.

"Yes, we are!" Coyote echoed. "So we must try to make daylight."

Turtle frowned. "How?" he asked.

But Jackrabbit leaped up in excitement. "Yes, yes, *yes!*"

"And perhaps we can get fire for all of the animal people," Coyote went on.

"Where?" Turtle asked.

Coyote grinned. "I know the place. Not long ago, I passed a cave in a high bank. When the little people there opened the door, some light spilled out. They were the Bug People, and inside their cave I saw fire. It made the cave as bright as day, but then the people shut the door again. They only open it up for their own people to come in. Their fire is only for themselves."

Black Hawk, Jackrabbit, Prairie Chicken, and Turtle scowled and muttered when they heard that.

"Now," said Coyote, "how are we going to get it?"

Black Hawk and Prairie Chicken piped up together. "We can see you have a plan," they said. "Tell us."

Coyote puffed out his chest a little. "It is this," he said. "I will go along to that cave to spy out how they guard their fire. I want to see who guards the door. You must follow behind, and wait where I tell you."

So the five of them set out.

When they had gone a little way, Coyote said to Turtle, "Wait here," and went on with the others. "Wait here," Coyote said to Prairie Chicken after a while. Jackrabbit was left behind next, and Black Hawk last. Coyote went on alone.

When he came near the place where he thought

the cave was, he sat down to watch and wait. After a while he saw a crack of light as a door began to open. The door in the hill swung out, and in the light that spilled through it, he saw one of the little bug people. It was Dragonfly. "What luck!" thought Coyote. Dragonfly could not turn his head, so he could look only straight ahead. All Coyote had to do was to creep up behind him to catch him.

So he did.

"*Skree-eek!*" squeaked Dragonfly. His wings fluttered in fright.

Coyote growled softly. "Hoh, you! What are you doing out here?"

"Watching!" Dragonfly squeaked. "Only watching. I watch the door to be sure that only Bug People go in. I can see only straight ahead, so the people know I am a good watcher. My eyes never wander. If I say 'Open the door,' they open it."

Coyote grinned. "Good. And I have you now, little bug! Shall I squash you or let you go? If you will call out to the people to open the door, I will set you free."

"Then they will kill me!" Dragonfly squeaked.

Coyote shrugged. "You can fly away. They cannot see you in the dark." He gave Dragonfly a little pinch.

"*Aow!*" Dragonfly shrieked, and quickly called out, "You people inside! Open the door!" Then, as

soon as Coyote let him go, he skittered away into the darkness.

The door opened. Inside Coyote saw a large, bright room, a bright fire set in a circle of stones, and all of the Bug People dancing. They laughed and hopped and twirled. Everyone else on the earth was miserable, but the Bug People were happy and dancing. Coyote stepped in.

The people stopped dancing. "Hoh, Big One!" they cried. "How did you get in? Who let you in?"

"I let myself in," Coyote said. "Oh, please, good people, let me stay! I love dancing. I will work for you—I will carry the food to your cooks by the fire—if only I can join in your dance."

The Bug People were still feeling happy from the dancing, so they squeaked, "Very well. Come in and shut the door and dance."

The people laughed when they saw Coyote's wild dancing. He skipped and bobbed and whirled, coming closer to the fire with each twirl.

"Look out!" the Bug People called. "Your tail will catch fire! Your tail will catch fire!"

Coyote laughed and whirled again. "I don't care! I love to dance!"

He danced and danced, and then, when he was close enough to the fire, he put his tail right into it, scooped up coals and flame with it, and dashed for the door. The Bug People chased after him. They shouted to one another, "Stop him! Stop him! Stop him!"

Coyote ran so fast that it was not long before he grew tired. He was almost at the place where Black Hawk was waiting, so he called out, "Hawk! Hawk!"

Black Hawk swooped down, took up the coals on his own tail, and flew off with the Bug People whizzing behind. He drew as far ahead as he could, and when he came to the place where Jackrabbit waited, he passed the fire to him. Jackrabbit ran until he, too, was tired. Then Prairie Chicken took the fire from him, and flew with it to meet Turtle. The Bug People were so close behind by then that Turtle only had time to shut himself inside his shell with the coals.

"Open up! Open up!" cried the Bug People. They knocked on Turtle's shell. They shouted at the place where only the beak over his mouth showed. They rocked his shell back and forth. Nothing would make him come out.

"Roll him down into the river!" called some. So they did. Turtle rolled over and over, plopped into the water, and sank. The Bug People waited for a while, but at last they gave up and went home.

Coyote and Black Hawk, Jackrabbit and Prairie Chicken had come up just as Turtle rolled into the water. They hid in the tall grass until the Bug

People were gone, then ran to help Turtle out of the stream. Then they gathered some wood and made a big fire with the coals Turtle had saved.

"Now," Coyote asked, "what shall we do with fire?" And he answered himself, "*I* think we should make daylight."

His companions agreed, for that was why they had come in the first place. "You know how. You make it," they said. So Coyote took the fire and rolled it into a sun, and suddenly everything around was bright with daylight.

Coyote was pleased with himself. "Good! Now, where will we put it?"

Before Coyote could answer his own question again, Black Hawk and Prairie Chicken flew up to the top of the highest mountain. "Up here! Let us put it up here," they called.

"No," Coyote shouted back. "The people who live too far away to see the mountain will not be able to see it there." He turned to the sun. "Sun, I am going to throw you up into the sky. Up there you can roll around and give daylight to everyone."

Coyote did just that. Coyote's companions cheered as Sun shone out across the world, but Coyote was not finished. Some fire still was left.

"What shall we do with this last bit?" Coyote asked. The others waited for him to answer himself, and he did. "I say we should put fire into rocks, and give rocks to everyone."

So he did, and today fire rocks still hold fire. People still can strike two fire rocks together, and with tinder and dry wood make a fire for cooking and keeping warm. And the Bug People cannot steal it back.

WHY BEAR WADDLES
WHEN HE WALKS

Comanche

In the First Days of the World, Sun did not travel
the path it travels now. Sometimes he soared and
swooped across the sky like a great golden bird.
Sometimes he was high and sometimes low. At
times he stood in one place until the leaves of the
trees on the earth below turned yellow and the
prairie grass grew brown.

"Will night never come?" the night animals
growled then. "How can we hunt when every mouse
can see us coming?"

But when Sun moved on and night did come,
the darkness might stay for days or weeks. The earth
grew cold and everything green stopped growing.

"Will the day never come?" the day animals
chattered as they shivered together.

At last everyone grew so weary and hungry that
they decided to hold a great council of all of the
animals to talk about what to do. Sun had traveled
over the edge of the world and stopped there that
day, so there was still light to see by. In the twilight
the animals drew a great circle in the earth and

brought the trunks of fallen trees to set around it for benches.

It was Coyote who stepped forward first to speak. He puffed up his chest and spoke as if he were the chief. "We must do something about the sun," he said. "The way things are now, no one is happy, day or night. I say, either we day animals ought to have it, or the night animals ought to get rid of it altogether."

Almost everyone in the council circle nodded and muttered, but Scissor-Tailed Flycatcher spoke up. *"Keck-keck-kew!"* he cried. "How can we do that? How can we tell Sun where to go? Sun is stronger than any of us. He is stronger than all of us together!"

But no one listened. Scissor-Tailed Flycatcher was always twittering and chattering.

"I know!" Bear boomed. He sat up straight on his bench and beamed. "We can play the hand game for it! The winning side can keep the sun or hide it away, whichever it likes."

"Yes, yes, the hand game!" everyone cried. "We can play the hand game for it!"

One ran to fetch the guessing bones for the players to hide in their hands. Another hurried to bring a bundle of crow-feathered pointing wands for the guessers to use to point to their guesses. A third dashed off to find twenty painted dogwood sticks for the scorers to keep score with. Each of the two sides chose one of their number to umpire the game as scorer. The day side chose Coyote. The night side chose Owl.

Coyote and Owl went off to pick a big, flat rock for their table. When they found a good one, they placed their counting sticks on it. The other animals brought the log benches and set them out in two long lines facing each other. The two scorers sat at one end with their flat rock between them.

The day animals played first. Rabbit and Fox, at the head of the line of day animals, started off. Nighthawk, across from them, was first guesser for the night side. The players held out the guessing bones, one in each hand or claw or paw, to show to those on the other side. One short bone was plain, and the other, the lucky bone, had a narrow cord wound around its middle. The players on the night side leaned forward to see which paws held the lucky bones.

Then Rabbit and Fox closed their paws and began to move them back and forth so fast that it was hard for even the fastest eyes to tell which paws held the bones. Then one of Fox's paws touched his neighbor Lizard's long-fingered hand. Lizard's fingers closed, and his hands began to flash to and fro. Then Hawk joined in, and soon, to confuse the guessers, paws and hands and hooves and claws flashed all along the line. They passed their hands behind their backs. The nearest waved their paws under the guessers' noses. The night animals' eyes flickered back and forth, chasing the lucky bones. At last Bat pointed his guessing wands at Buffalo and Mouse.

"No!" they cried. Buffalo showed his empty hooves, and Mouse his empty paws. The hands began to fly again, but this time the guesser was Mole, whose eyes were sharpest at dusk. He pointed his guessing wands at Scissor-Tailed Flycatcher and Hawk. Each held a lucky bone. A score for the night people! Owl moved a scoring stick to the night side of the stone table.

Then it was the night side's turn to take the bones, and the game went on. And on. And on. Both sides were so clever at the game that a long time passed between good guesses. The guessing bones went from the night side to the day side and back again as first one team was lucky, and then the other. Sun had at last gone to bed below the edge of the world and lay there listening to hear what the animals decided to do with him. He began to be tired of waiting.

Still the game went on and on.

Bear grew tired, too. He was sitting on the night side because he loved to sleep through the dark winter. The bench was low, and he was not used to sitting upright. His legs ached, and his feet were swollen. He kicked off his moccasins. That helped a little, but still the game went on.

Sun had had enough, though. What was happening? He had to know. He rolled out of bed and stretched himself to full size, then began to climb his ladder toward the top side of the world. In the world above the sky in the east began to glow.

"Kee-ick!" Nighthawk croaked. "The sun is coming!"

The frightened night animals jumped to their feet. "Run! Run!" they cried, and they ran.

Bear sprang to his feet and hopped off just as Sun popped up into the sky. He pulled on his moccasins as he hopped, but his left foot went into his right moccasin, and his right foot went into the left. The other night animals headed west toward the woods or to their dens in the earth. Bear hurried after them as fast as he could, but his feet hurt in the wrong moccasins. He waddled from side to side as he went, and roared.

"Ouch! Wait! Ouch-*ouch*! Oh, wait for me!" he roared as he waddled westward, away from the sun.

He has been waddling ever since.

Since no one had won the hand game, it was decided that, from that day on, day and night would take turns. The day people and the night people could take turns at living just as they wished.

And so everyone could be happy half of the time.

THE QUARREL BETWEEN WIND AND THUNDER

Lipan Apache

At sunrise, Wind and Thunder looked over the bright, new earth and saw that it was a good place to live.

Wind puffed out his chest. "My earth! How proud of it I am! After all, I am the one who works to keep it trim and beautiful. I *should* be proud!"

"You?" Thunder rumbled in fury. "I am the one who should be proud. I am the one who keeps the earth as it should be. I, not you, you . . . you sack of wind!"

Thunder was so angry that he could not listen to any more of Wind's bragging or even bear the sight of him. He stomped away, crashing and booming all the way up the sky.

Once Thunder was out of hearing, Wind said to himself, "Poh! The earth does not need that bad-tempered fellow. *I* don't need him. I shall keep this beautiful earth neat and green by myself. I shall make the grass greener, the blooms brighter, the trees taller. Let him watch and see!"

So wind began to blow. "Grow, grow!" he sang

as he blew. He blew and he blew and he *BLEW*! But no grass or flowers or trees grew. Every day the earth was more brown and parched. The lakes and creeks began to shrink. Wind grew frightened at last and knew that he would have to search the sky to find Thunder.

When he found him, he said, "I was wrong, Thunder. I cannot take care of the earth alone. We must be brothers again, and work together. Without you, I have worked hard, but everywhere I have made the earth dry and brown. Will you come down with me so that we may heal it?"

Thunder was pleased, and he hurried back down the sky with Wind. He growled and grumbled and roared as he went, so that the clouds grew dark, and the rain rained down. Here, the grass grew high. There, the yucca plants bloomed. Along the streambeds cottonwood trees sprouted new green leaves. Wind followed Thunder and his rain across the earth, and was happy again as he blew through the high grass.

So it was that the two became brothers again, and work together still.

Thunderbird Woman, Skiwis, and Little Big-Belly Boy

Waco

Three friends—Thunderbird Woman, Skiwis, and Little Big-Belly Boy—lived together in Thunderbird Woman's big grass lodge. The lodge was made of bundles of long grass tightly woven onto a willow framework. It had a door on the north side, and a door on the south side. A large cottonwood tree grew by the north door and gave them shade in the summer. Thunderbird Woman, Skiwis, and Little Big-Belly Boy shared the work among them. Thunderbird Woman did the cooking and gathered the firewood. Skiwis, who was a big, strong man, did all the hunting, and Little Big-Belly Boy carried up from the creek all the water for drinking and cooking and washing. They lived happily together there for a long time.

Once when Skiwis was out hunting, a blade of grass dropped onto his back while he was bending over a buffalo's tracks. He tried and tried, but he could not straighten up again, for though he was strong enough to lift a buffalo, somehow he never could lift small things. For Skiwis a feather was as heavy as a buffalo would have been for Thunderbird Woman.

"Help!" he called. "Little Big-Belly Boy, wherever you are, come help me!"

Little Big-Belly Boy, when he came, laughed to see the big man groan under the weight of the grass. Instead of helping, he decided to have some fun. He sat down on the ground, frowned, and said, "But Skiwis, it is only a blade of grass. If you shrug, it will fall off."

"I cannot," Skiwis wheezed. "Help me, or it will crush me to the ground!"

But for every time the big man pleaded, "Help me!" the boy answered, "But, Skiwis . . ." At last, when Skiwis collapsed on the ground, Little Big-Belly Boy picked the blade of grass from his back.

"Ai-ee!" Skiwis cried out as he struggled to his feet. "I cannot hunt with so sore a back. You must come home with me and help me cure it."

So they went together back to the grass lodge. There, Skiwis uprooted a cottonwood tree from the grove along the creek, lay face down, and tugged the tree onto his back so that it stood upright on its roots. "Go gather firewood," he said to Little Big-Belly Boy, "and pile it up atop the tree roots, then light it. The heat will cure my soreness."

When the fire grew too hot, Skiwis shrugged it

off his back, and stood and stretched. "Much better," he said.

The next morning he went out hunting again, and did not return until late at night. With him he brought, on a strong grass rope, a large buffalo that he had caught and not killed. He led the angry beast to the north door of the grass lodge, listened to be sure that Thunderbird Woman and Little Big-Belly Boy were asleep, and tied the rope to the cottonwood tree there. In the morning, when the boy rose, took up a water jar, and went to go out, he found his way barred by the big buffalo. The *very* big buffalo. It bellowed.

Little Big-Belly Boy backed back into the lodge. "Skiwis, Skiwis!" he cried. "Help me! A big buffalo is standing here!"

Skiwis lay on his bed and pretended to be asleep. To tease Little Big-Belly Boy, he yawned and grunted, and turned onto his other side, with his face to the wall.

"Skiwis, Skiwis! Help me! Come and chase this big buffalo away!"

Skiwis only pulled his buffalo-robe blanket over his head, but his bed shook with his laughter. Little Big-Belly Boy came close and called out loudly into his ear, "Skiwis, Skiwis!"

Skiwis sat up and rubbed his ear.

"Skiwis, come kill this buffalo," the boy begged.

"Kill it and take the hide, and make for me a buffalo robe like yours."

So Skiwis did. He rose, stepped out, took the buffalo by the horns, gave it a great shake, and—*hai!*—was holding a handsome buffalo robe.

Little Big-Belly Boy thanked him for it, but thought to himself that he would frighten Skiwis to pay Skiwis for frightening him. A few days later, he caught a mouse and tied a thin hide cord around its neck. That night he tied the other end of the cord around the trunk of the cottonwood tree outside the lodge door. In the morning Skiwis rose early, but when he went to go out, he backed away from the doorway when he saw the mouse, for he was afraid of it. "Boy! Little Big-Belly Boy! Help me!" he cried. "There is a mouse here."

Then, "Come kill this mouse," he called.

Little Big-Belly Boy only lay in his bed and laughed. When at last he rose, Skiwis asked him to make him a mouse robe, as he had made the buffalo robe. So Little Big-Belly Boy did. That night, though, when Skiwis went to bed, he had to ask the boy's help to pull on his mouse robe, for it was too heavy for him. In the night, he could not turn over in his bed because of its weight, and had to call Little Big-Belly Boy to pull it off before he could sleep.

As the months passed, though, the boy grew

more quiet, the teasing and playing stopped, and Skiwis saw that he was unhappy. "Why are you unhappy?" Skiwis asked.

Little Big-Belly Boy shivered. "I had a telling-dream," he said. "A terrible creature is going to come and carry me off."

"Poh!" said Skiwis. "Let it try! I will shoot it dead, like this." He took up his bow and arrows, and when he shot at the tree in front of the grass house, the arrow went all the way through the tree.

"It will not be enough," the boy said. "The creature that will come has powers too great for you."

"Do not be afraid," Skiwis said. "I will find some way to protect you."

The creature came when Little Big-Belly Boy was out playing. He saw nothing, but heard a great rushing in the air, and ran as fast as he could to the grass lodge. "It is coming! I hear it!" he cried.

Skiwis went to the door. He looked, and saw a dark cloud sweeping down from the north. He looked again, and saw that the cloud was not a cloud, but a great, dark bird. When the bird came closer still, he saw that it had sharp flint stones all over its body instead of feathers, and a beak as hard and sharp as flint. It was Sun Buzzard, a monster from the fiery darkness at the back of the sun, and it swooped down heavily to light in the top of the big cottonwood tree.

Skiwis took up his bow and arrows, and stepped outside. He shot, and missed. Four times he shot. Four times he missed. When he had shot his last arrow, Sun Buzzard flew down with an angry scream, seized Skiwis in its beak, tossed him onto its stone-feathered back, and flew away. It flew far across the land until it came to a great, wide stretch of water, and then on across the water toward a small island. The sharp stones cut Skiwis's hands, but he hung on until Sun Buzzard reached around with its beak and pulled him off. It swooped down and dropped him into a nest in the top of the tallest tree on the island.

Hai! I am safe for a while, Skiwis thought when he looked up and saw Sun Buzzard flap away. He looked down over the edge of the nest and saw heaps of bones on the ground far below, and as he looked, he felt a sharp bite on his foot. When he rolled over, he saw four young buzzards with fuzz instead of feathers. "Meat, meat!" they squeaked. They began to peck at him.

"*HOH!*" Skiwis roared in his loudest voice. The young buzzards tumbled over one another as they backed toward the far side of the nest. Skiwis reached out and snatched up one by its neck. "HOH!" he roared again to keep the others away. "You all are too small to be Sun Buzzard's children. Whose children are you?"

"I am the child of Nice Clear Weather," piped up one.

"And I of Hard Rain Followed by Hard Wind," squeaked another.

"And I of Foggy Day."

"And I of Cold Weather Followed by Blizzard," croaked the one he held.

"People don't want *you*," Skiwis exclaimed, and he threw it out of the nest. Then he threw out the child of Hard Rain Followed by Hard Wind. "You two may stay," he said to the children of Nice Clear Weather and Foggy Day as he climbed over the edge of the nest and started down the tree. "Everyone likes nice, clear weather, and *I* like foggy days."

When he reached the ground, Skiwis took the bowstring from his bow and stretched it out longer and longer until he thought that it was long enough to reach across the water to the far shore. Then he swung the string back and with a mighty *thwack!* struck out and down with it like a whip. Out the string flew, and down it snapped with such a mighty blow that the water sprang up and away on both sides. Swiftly, Skiwis jumped down from the island and ran along the muddy bottom before the waters on the two sides could rush back together. When he reached the shore, he kept on running so that he could reach his own country and grass lodge, and Thunderbird Woman and Little

Big-Belly Boy, before Sun Buzzard discovered he was gone.

For a long while all was well, but at last Sun Buzzard did come. The three friends in the grass lodge heard its scream and the noise as it settled down atop the big cottonwood tree beside the north door. Skiwis shook with fright. Seeing his fear, Little Big-Belly Boy grew even more frightened.

"Come," Thunderbird Woman said. "I know what to do. Follow me." She led them out the south door and on toward the mountains not far off. When they reached the mountains, Thunderbird Woman took Skiwis and the boy up on her back and carried them straight into the rock. A way opened up before her as she went, and the rock closed up behind her. When they came out on the other side of the mountains, she sat down to rest.

"Go, Skiwis. Put your ear to the mountain and tell us whether Sun Buzzard is coming still."

Skiwis went to put his ear to the rock and heard a far-off grinding sound. "It is coming," he called.

The others came close to listen as Sun Buzzard slowly ground his way through the rock. When at last it broke through the side of the mountain, it fell flat. Unlike Thunderbird Woman, it had no magical power. Its great strength and anger alone had brought it through the rock. Its beak was broken off. Most of the stones it wore in place of feathers were torn away. Its wings were ripped. But still it shrieked and lunged at Skiwis, until he lifted up and dropped a great rock on it, and killed it.

"Monsters!" said Thunderbird Woman. "But now all is well again." And she took Skiwis and the boy back up on her back, and set out through the rock mountain for home.

THE MONSTERS AND THE FLOOD

Wichita

One day, in a village in the Early Days of the World country, four creatures shaped like puppies were born. When they were one day old, they were twice as big as the day before. When they were three days old, they had grown large and strong enough to play with the children and run all around the camp. And they kept on growing. The bigger they became, the meaner they grew. Soon the children were afraid of them. At first their parents only worried and chased the dogs away. After a while, when the dogs had grown as tall as the tipis, the people went to the chief to complain about the damage the monster puppies had done to their homes and their fields of maize. The chief grew weary of hearing complaints all day. "I hear, I hear. We will send the pups away," the chief said. And he told four of the men to tie ropes around the necks of the dogs and lead them away to the west, to leave them there.

The men led the giant dogs away to the west, but never returned, for the dogs ate them up. When four more men went out to look for the first four, they saw that the dogs were dogs no longer. They had grown long necks. That was all the men had time to see, for the monsters stretched out their long necks and swallowed them up. When still more people came to look for their friends, they were snapped up and gobbled down too.

At last the people of the village understood how dreadful the dogs had grown, and they were frightened. The old people wailed that though the Creator had made all that was good, it seemed now that He had made monsters to destroy them all. It seemed that every day was worse than the day before. They were so frightened that everyone except one old man and woman and their grandson packed up their belongings and moved the village a day's journey away. They never again went west to the place where the monsters lived.

The old man and woman and their grandson, whose name was Of Unknown Father, did not wish to move. They stayed in their lodge at the northeast corner of the old village so that the mysterious father of Of Unknown Father would know where to send his messengers to find the boy. They were right to stay, for that night a messenger came. He told the boy to come the next day at midday to a certain hill to the north. The next day, the boy went at noon to that place, and saw the same messenger waiting for him.

"I am sent with a warning from your father in

the Sky Country," the man said. "He is unhappy that monsters and wickedness have come into the world. He has decided that he must destroy this world and begin again. You are to go to the chief's new village and tell the people that all will be destroyed. If they do not listen, tell them again."

"But if my father wishes to be rid of the monsters," said Of Unknown Father, "then I wish him to destroy them only, not all of the people."

"That is good," said the messenger, as if that was the best of all answers the boy could have made. "Then you must do four things now. You must gather twelve of the longest cane stalks you can find, and fasten them together. You must go to the village and give the bundle of canes to Spider Woman. You must tell Spider Woman to send her servant, Mouse Woman, to go about and gather seeds and dried corn of all colors. Then you must plant the canes in the ground up to the fifth joint. After four days, a great water will come, and in it something to destroy the monsters. Go now, and tell people that they must leave their villages and find places safe from the waters."

Of Unknown Father did as the messenger told him. He went first to the chief's village to warn the people of the flood that would come to destroy them and their lodges. The chief would not believe him. Only Spider Woman believed him.

Spider Woman took the twelve long canes that Of Unknown Father had cut and brought to her, and sent her servant, Mouse Woman, out with baskets to collect seeds and corn. When Mouse Woman returned with her baskets full, Spider Woman filled the first tall cane with kernels of corn, then closed the top with clay. The other canes she filled in turn with beans or pumpkin seeds or watermelon seeds, and every other seed Mouse Woman had found.

All that was left to do was to plant the canes in the ground. Spider Woman dug the hole. Of Unknown Father caused a wind to blow, and the wind raised the canes straight up. Spider Woman and the boy moved them to the hole and planted them up to the fifth joint. As soon as they had planted them, the sky began to dim, as if a dark cloud were blowing across it. But there was no wind. The cloud was all of the birds of the air fleeing to the south. Almost at once the earth began to thunder as herds of animals came sweeping down from the north. First came the buffalo people, then the deer, and after the bears came all of the smaller folk. Spider Woman ran to the canes and climbed up quickly to the top, then let down a rope and pulled up her husband. Next, she pulled up Of Unknown Father, and then Mouse Woman. Once they were safe, she spun a shelter to cover them.

When all of the animals had passed by below, Of Unknown Father and the others saw great floods of water following close behind them. Coming with the water was a great turtle which headed straight for the hillock of dry earth in the west where the four monsters stood. It burrowed under their feet and then rose up.

The monsters could not free themselves from its back. The waters grew deeper and inched up the turtle's shell. The monsters' feet slithered and slipped. In their fear of the water, they struggled to stand still, but the one at the tail end of the turtle fell into the water and drowned. On the second day, the monster on the far side fell in. On the third day, his brother nearest the turtle's head toppled in. On the fourth day, the last monster slid in and drowned. That is why the people who lived on earth from that time on gave the monsters' names to the four directions in which they fell. Their names were North, East, South, and West.

The floodwaters stayed for twelve more days. Of Unknown Father, Spider Woman and her husband, and Mouse Woman waited on their perch atop the canes. They saw no people or villages, only water, and here and there a little ground. Even the wind was still.

The wind was still, but from the Sky Country the one named Going All Around flew down.

He was one who could dry out mud faster than any wind. When he flew over the earth the first time, he saw an odd shadow shaped like a woman shining on the ground. He circled over the earth again and again, drying it out, and the next time he passed over that spot, he saw that the upper part of the shadow image in the mud was alive. It was alive and nursing a new child in its arms. When he passed over yet again, she was sitting up with the child in her lap.

Going All Around flew down and stood beside her. "Stand up and come with me, Shadow Woman," he commanded.

He led the woman to a great beaver lodge under the waters, where many people were living safe from the flood. For five days she and the baby son she called Standing Sweet Grass stayed there. In those five days Standing Sweet Grass grew into a boy who could run and talk, for he was the son of Man Above, not a man of this earth.

On his sixth day, Standing Sweet Grass left the beaver lodge and found Going All Around still at his work of drying out the earth. Together they came to the shallow waters where the people were perched atop the twelve tall canes.

"Hoh!" Spider Woman cried from above. "Look out for the boy coming down." And she let down Of Unknown Father on a rope.

When the boy reached the ground, Going All Around said to him, "You have power to command the winds. Use it now to help me dry the waters from this place."

To the surprise of Of Unknown Father, the four Winds came at his command, and soon the ground where the canes stood was dry. Spider Woman let down her husband and Mouse Woman on ropes, and then climbed down herself. When Spider Woman reached the ground, the boy Standing Sweet Grass spoke up.

"Come with me to my home," he said. "Many others who have lost their homes are living there. They will make you welcome."

So they went, and pulled up the long canes and carried them with them. The canes were so long that Of Unknown Father carried one end of the bundle, Mouse Woman the other, and Spider Woman and her husband the middle. When they went down to the beaver lodge, they saw a great crowd of birds and animals and people. Shadow Woman came to welcome them.

"Our gifts will be welcome too," said Of Unknown Father, and he and Spider Woman opened the canes and poured out the seeds. As the people began to divide the seeds among all of them, the boy said, "With these you can begin your life in the new world."

Shadow Woman's son, Standing Sweet Grass, gave them great thanks. "We will share these seeds out among all the people, so that they may eat and live."

And that, the Wichita say, is how it happened that the new world came to be green and growing, and full of people.

COYOTE AND THE SEVEN BROTHERS

Caddo

Long ago, an old woman lived with her seven sons in a lodge at the edge of the woods. All of her sons were fine hunters, and every evening they brought home more game than the eight of them could eat. The old woman was kept busy from sunrise to sunset cooking their meals and drying the meat they could not eat.

One day the old woman's eldest son went hunting and did not come home. After three days his dogs returned, but he did not.

The next day the old woman's second son said, "Do not worry, Mother. I will go and find my brother." And he took the dogs and set out. After three days the dogs came back, but neither he nor his brother were with them.

The third brother said, "Do not worry, Mother. I will go and find my brothers."

But, again, the dogs returned alone.

The fourth, fifth, and sixth brothers, each in turn, went out to search for his lost brothers, but each time the dogs came home days later alone.

"Mother," said Small Brother, the seventh son. "I must go and find my brothers."

But his mother was frightened. "No, no!" she cried. "You cannot! If you go, I will lose you, too. You will never return. You must not go."

Small Brother was sad, but he stayed at home. One day when his brothers had been gone for a long time, he was playing in front of the lodge when he saw a raccoon sitting in a tree at the edge of the woods.

"Mother, Mother!" he called. "A raccoon is sitting in a tree at the edge of the woods. If you will bring me my bow and arrows, we will have fresh meat tonight."

"I will," answered the old woman, and she brought out his bow and arrows.

Small Brother called the dogs. The raccoon saw the boy and the dogs coming, and jumped to the next tree, and the next and the next. Small Brother followed it deep into the woods, until at last it ran up a tree and down a big hole in its trunk. The boy climbed up and reached down into the tree to grasp the raccoon by the tail.

"Hoh, boy!" a strange voice called.

Small Brother looked down and saw a little old woman with a sharp, pointed nose.

"Drop the raccoon down here," the old woman said. "Your dogs and I will kill it." So Small Brother threw the raccoon down. The old woman killed it, but when he was not looking, she killed one of his dogs, too. "Look in the tree," she called. "There is another raccoon."

Small Brother looked, and there was, so he threw that one down to her. She killed that one too, and when he was not looking, she killed another dog.

"I see *another* raccoon," Small Brother called happily, and he reached down and pulled that one out, and threw it down to the old woman. Four . . . five . . . six raccoons he threw down, and the old woman killed them, and with each one, another dog. Small Brother was about to pull the seventh and last raccoon out from the hole in the tree when suddenly it spoke to him.

"Little boy," it said, "that old woman is a witch. It was she who killed your brothers. Now she has killed all of your dogs, and she will kill you next if you do not run. You must pull me out and throw me as far from the tree as you can. I will run off, and the old witch will chase me. Then you must run home as fast as your feet can fly."

Small Brother looked down and saw that it was so. All of his dogs were gone. "I will," he said. He threw the seventh raccoon as far as he could, jumped down from the tree, and ran away home.

The witch returned to the tree when she had found the last raccoon and killed it, and was angry to find the little boy gone. She chased after him, but he was so far ahead that she could not catch him.

The boy told his mother all that had happened. That night he had a strange dream. In the morning he told the dream to his mother. "In the dream," he said, "I was walking along, and I met Coyote. He told me that my brothers are not dead. A wicked chief and his people captured them and made them slaves. They must work so hard that they will die if they do not get away. And, Mother, Coyote promised to help!"

"Then he will," said his old mother.

That afternoon Small Brother went out hunting. Just as in his dream, he met Coyote as he was walking along. Just as in his dream, Coyote told him that his brothers were not dead.

"A wicked chief and his people have captured them and made them their slaves," Coyote said. "They must work so hard that they will die if they do not get away, so I am on my way to help them."

Small Brother went home to tell his mother, and Coyote went on through the woods. Soon he spied Flying Squirrel. Flying Squirrel was hard at work filling a big basket with pecan nuts.

"Give me some pecans, friend," Coyote said. "You have too big a load to fly with."

"Then I must drag it," Flying Squirrel answered. He gave a nervous look over his shoulder. "The pecans are for Wicked Chief, who is my master. I cannot give you even one."

Coyote was pleased. "Hoh! You're just the fellow I was looking for. What is your master like? And does he still have six brothers for servants, and are they well?"

Flying Squirrel chattered away at great speed. He told Coyote that Wicked Chief was a monster with a long, pointed beak of a nose, that he lived across the wide river, that his people were almost as bad as he, and that the six brothers were still alive, but if the bad people killed them, they would eat them.

"Hoh! Well, I am here to help those brothers get away. Your monster chief cannot be as clever as I, and I have great magic," Coyote bragged. "All I need is a way to cross the wide river."

"If you hold on to my tail as I fly, I will take you across," Flying Squirrel offered.

"I can do that," Coyote said. So, off they went, soaring over the river, but Flying Squirrel's tail was so silky smooth that Coyote's paws began to slip. He slip-slip-slipped right off the end of it just before they reached the far bank of the river, and he fell into the water. He crawled out and hid in the tall grass to shake himself dry, and to think. "Hah!" he said to himself at last. "I will turn myself into a new corn grinder!"

So he did. The new hollowed-out stone grinding mill and its grinder stone slithered into the river and floated down to Wicked Chief's camp. Before long one of the women of the bad people came down to the riverbank with her water jar, and saw the mill.

"Hoh! I could use that," she said. When she could not reach it, she ran back to ask Wicked Chief to get it for her.

"A stone corn mill that floats?" the monster snorted. "Someone is playing a trick. It must be Coyote."

"I say it is a corn mill, and a fine one," the woman shouted. "And I want it."

The chief grumbled, but he sent someone to fish the corn mill out of the river. All of the bad women liked it so much that they took turns pounding their corn in it. "It is the best mill we have ever had," they said.

But the next day, the first bad woman was grinding fine sweet corn and looked down to see that all of her corn was gone. She dropped the grinder and ran to tell the chief.

"I told you that mill was Coyote," Wicked Chief growled. "Bring it to me."

When the woman brought it, he set it on the big log where he skewered prisoners with his long, spiked nose. "Take that, Coyote!" the monster crowed as he raised up his head and speared down with his nose. But as he did, the corn mill rolled off the log and turned into Coyote. Wicked Chief's nose was stuck so deep into the log that it never came out, and he could never move.

Coyote called together all of the slaves and told them they were free. Then he sent the six brothers home to their mother and Small Brother. Always afterward, when the seven brothers killed any game for their dinner, they left a share of the meat behind for Coyote.

SLAYING THE MONSTERS

Kadohadacho

In the First Time, it seemed that the world was full of horrible, terrible wild creatures. They were fierce hunters, and all of the animal people lived in fear of them. At last, Coyote called a council of all the animal people, to talk of what they must do to be rid of the monsters and their fear. The people had grown so afraid that they stayed in their lodges instead of going out to hunt. They were afraid to go out to gather food, or to visit friends.

The animals gathered in a great crowd at the center of a wide plain of grass, and sat themselves down in rows in a circle. The grass was as tall as trees, and hid them well from the monsters. There they talked and listened and argued for hours, but at last they agreed.

"At last we are agreed," Coyote said. "We will set fire to the tall grass, and the grass will set fire to the trees, and the trees will set fire to the world. Now— who will fly up to the sky to find a star where we can live while the earth burns?"

"White-Headed Hawk!" cried the birds. "He has the swiftest wings of us all."

"No, Crow! Crow should go!" called the other

people. "For he is the cleverest talker of all the winged folk."

Both White-Headed Hawk and Crow were willing to go, so the people decided that the two of them should fly up to the sky together. They decided that they should leave at once. So they did, and high up in the sky they found a friendly star. Crow told him of the monsters and the council, and that all of the people would have to come live in the sky.

"You are welcome to come," Star answered. "There is room enough here in the sky for all of you. But how will you set the whole earth on fire? And how will those without wings fly up to the sky?"

White-Headed Hawk and Crow did not know, but they flew back down to the council in the tall grass and told everyone all that Star had said. The people talked it over, and decided that runners could set the fires, and that those without wings would climb up to the sky on a rope.

At once they set out to gather soapweed for a rope, keeping watch all of the time for monsters. When they had enough soapweed, many of them worked to twist it into cords, and the best rope makers braided the cords into rope. To take fire around the world, the people chose Black Snake and Gray Snake, for they were the fastest runners. Carrying coals of fire on their tails, they were to start out at the same time. One would go toward the Far North, and one to the Far South. "Then," they said, "we will run to the West, and return together from there."

Once the two snakes were on their way, everyone worked hard to finish the rope. From time to time while they worked, Pigeon would fly high into the sky to watch for signs of fire.

"I see smoke to the north, and down to the south," he called to the people below.

"I see smoke to the west," he called after a while.

"I see smoke coming this way," he called later still.

Soon the people did not need Pigeon to warn them to hurry, for the blue sky had turned gray with smoke. The rope makers' fingers flew at their work, and the rope grew longer and longer. No sooner was it finished than Black Snake and Gray Snake returned. At once White-Headed Hawk and Crow took hold of the rope and flew with it back up to the sky country, to Star. Star fastened down the end of it with a great rock, and let the rest hang straight down toward Earth. It was a beautiful rope, and it was so long that it reached all the way.

The fire came swiftly, and with it all the monsters running before it and roaring. The sky was red and black as the birds flew up and the others climbed onto the rope. Soon all of the people were safely on the rope, but the monsters crowded around and began climbing too.

In the sky above, Star hauled up on the rope, and before long the first of the animal people climbed onto the sky country. "Hurry! Hurry!" they cried to the bird people. "Someone with sharp teeth must fly down to cut the rope!"

But none of the birds had teeth.

"I have teeth!" cried Bat, and he swooped over the edge and down. When he had flown down as far as the last animal climber, he perched on the rope just below him and began to bite at it.

"R-rhoh, you! Leather Wings!" the first monster below roared up at him as it climbed. "What are you eating there?"

"Nothing, nothing!" Bat chattered. "Only some corn my grandmother parched for me." He chewed away busily as the monsters climbed nearer and nearer. Just in time, he cut the last cord. The rope fell away, and the monsters dropped with it.

Bat flew down through the smoke to make sure they were all roasted in the fire. But they were not.

"*Skree-eek!*" he squeaked in alarm, for just below, he saw a monster that was bigger than all of the other monsters together. The other monsters were crawling into its huge nose and great, gaping mouth to escape the fire.

Clever Bat—brave Bat—waited until all of the

monsters were inside. Then he flew down into the chief monster's nose and pulled out a pawful of hairs.

The great monster drew a deep breath of smoke—"*HRAHR-AH*"—and sneezed out all of the other monsters into the flames—"**CHOO!**" And he and they burned up together.

Bat himself was scorched a little, which is why his wings are the color of dark smoke, but he flew safely up to the sky country. Once all of the monsters were burned up, the animal and bird people returned to the earth, and the earth has been a good home to them ever since.

HOLD UP THE SKY

Lipan Apache

Coyote was out walking one morning, enjoying the fine day, when he passed a giant yucca plant. At the top of the plant was a stalk, and at the top of the stalk was a tasty-looking lizard.

"Aho!" said Coyote to himself. "Already I have a fine day. Now I am about to have a fine bite to eat!" Silently, he rose up on his hind legs and opened his mouth wide.

Lizard smelled his breath. She swiveled an eye around and saw the sharp teeth almost near enough to bite. "Coyote! Just in time!" she shouted. "Here, hold up the sky!"

Coyote blinked, and pulled back a little in surprise.

"Are you blind?" Lizard scolded. "Don't you see that I am propping up this stalk, which holds up the sky? You have come just in time. I have been holding it up all day, and was just about to fall off. Quickly! Take hold of it just below me, and I will run to fetch my children. They can take the next turn."

Coyote was alarmed. He reached out and grasped the stalk in both paws. "Take care," he warned Lizard as she scrambled down. "Do not fall." He watched her until she reached the rocks nearby and disappeared into a crack.

The day was very hot. The sun beat down on Coyote's head. As he grew hotter and hotter, he began to pant. He grew tired and at last called out to Lizard, "Hai, Lizard! Where are you?"

Lizard was watching from the shadow between two big rocks. She grinned.

Coyote became so tired that his stretched-out arms began to tremble. "Lizard!" he shouted. "Where are you? The sun is roasting me, and my arms are tired. Make your children hurry!"

Lizard sat still and laughed into her hands.

Coyote looked around in a panic. Lizard and her children were nowhere in sight. What he did see was a little gully that rainwater had made on its way to the creek. "Perhaps," he thought, "if I run as fast as I can, I can reach the gully before the sky falls. It is deep enough. I should be safe there." He eyed the sky.

"It isn't my fault," he shouted up toward the sky country. "This isn't *my* job!"

Then he let go and ran. He ran faster than he had ever run before, and threw himself into the gully. After a moment he looked up and saw that the sky had not yet fallen. He might have time to reach the next gully. He scrambled out and ran on, and rolled safely into the next one.

Lizard laughed so hard that she had to roll over and kick her legs in the air.

Coyote was four gullies away from the giant yucca plant before he caught on. "'The sky is falling,' indeed!" he snorted. Lizard had fooled him. He kicked at a stone in disgust. "She only wanted to get away!"

Lizard went home to tell her children about her adventure. Together, she and the little lizards laughed so hard that they *all* had to roll over and kick their little legs in the air.

COYOTE AND MOUSE

Tonkawa

Mouse and her six children lived happily in a tidy little tipi in the shelter of a bumelia bush. Each morning when the sun rose, Mouse awoke and sang her song. Her children woke to its twitter, and danced to its tune. They could not help themselves. It was that sort of song. The words were homely, about sunshine and showers, or bramble berries and buffalo clover, and the tune leaped and pranced so happily that the little mice had to leap and prance too. As the sun warmed the earth, Mouse went out each morning to collect seeds. She took her children with her, and while she searched, she sang her special song, and they danced. When she had filled her basket with seeds, she sang all the way home, and her children danced home after her.

One morning, Coyote came trotting out for a walk. Being Coyote, he had his ears up, eyes out, and nose sniffing for anything curious he might poke his nose into, or any mischief he might stir up. When he heard the little song, he slowed, cocked an ear, and followed it. He couldn't help dancing along as he went. When the song led at last to the small tipi, Coyote edged closer to peer around the door flap. He saw Mouse setting out her children's morning meal, and still singing her song.

Coyote dropped the door flap. "You, Mouse!" he called out. "That song you are singing? Give it to me!"

"My song?" Mouse exclaimed inside the tipi. "No! It is mine."

"No more," Coyote said with a grin as he raised the door flap again. "I said, give it to me."

"I have never given my song to anyone," Mouse said. "Why should I give it to you?"

Coyote bared his teeth. "Because I want it."

Mouse began to be frightened, but she spoke up bravely. "It is my song. I made it for my children to dance to. It belongs to me, not to just anyone who asks for it."

Coyote grew angry. A *mouse*? Saying no to Coyote? Never! "*Give. It. To. Me!*" he growled.

Mouse trembled. "Very well. But you must wait a moment. We put it away when you called. We will fetch it."

With her children, she went down a hole in the tipi floor. Coyote paced up and down as he waited. After a little while he called out, "Come out of there!"

Mouse did not answer.

Coyote went to listen at the hole, and heard nothing. He dug furiously, but he found nothing.

Mouse and her children had gone down one hole, come out through another, and escaped into the tall grass. All Coyote could do was growl and go home without a single note to sing.

COYOTE AND THE SMALLEST SNAKE

Tawakoni

One morning Coyote awoke in such a good mood that he felt as strong as a buffalo and as clever as three owls. He ate, took a drink of water from the creek, then trotted off toward the prairie. *"Hah! How lucky I am that I am I!"* he sang to himself as he went.

He had not gone far when he spied a tiny little snake wriggling along ahead of him. He laughed as he passed by. "Good morning, poor little Hissquawasedikis, poor little Ever Grows Larger, who never grows larger!"

Little Hissquawasedikis, the smallest of all the snakes, stopped. "Why 'poor'?" he called after Coyote.

"Why?" Coyote turned back, astonished. "How can you ask? Surely you dream of being as large and handsome as I! I know I would be ashamed to be as small and hairless as you. And as for my teeth . . ." He grinned. "Let me see *your* teeth, Little Hiss."

The smallest snake opened his mouth, and Coyote gave a scornful sniff. "You see! Now look at mine." He gave a great, sharp-toothed laugh. "Shall we play a game and bite each other? I would hardly feel your bite, but mine could cut you in two with one sharp snap. Just a pinch would finish you off!" Without waiting for the little snake to agree to his game, he bent down and gave Hissquawasedikis a sharp nip in his middle.

The surprised little snake gave Coyote a tiny bite on one paw and then tried to wriggle away. With a bend in his middle from Coyote's bite, all he could do was flop sideways off the path.

"I told you so, Little Hiss," Coyote said smugly. "I will just sit over here on the other side of this buckthorn bush where I won't bother you, and wait until you are all right again." That was a lie, of course, for Coyote disliked snakes. He was sure that Hissquawasedikis would die.

After a little while, Coyote called out loudly, "Are you still there?"

"Still here!" the smallest snake wheezed.

A little later, Coyote licked at his paw and called again. "Are you still there?" and the little snake called back weakly, "Still here."

Coyote's paw had begun to swell, but he grinned when only a whispered "Still here" answered his third call.

"I knew my nip would kill that snake," he said to himself, but he saw that his whole leg was swollen. It began to hurt. After a while he squeezed his eyes shut and called out again. He scowled when the smallest snake still quavered, "Still here." His whole body began to swell, but he kept on calling. "He ought to be dead by now," he thought each time. But as they called back and forth, Coyote's voice grew fainter, and the little snake's grew louder. "STILL HERE!"

When Coyote did not call again, the smallest snake shouted out, "ARE YOU STILL THERE?" When no answer came back, little Hissquawasedikis shut his eyes, clenched his jaw, and gave a great wiggle that straightened him out. Then he went over to take a look at Coyote.

Coyote lay on his back, swollen up as round as a giant puffball, with his legs in the air.

The smallest snake shook his head. "Silly braggart! Everyone knows that the name Ever Grows Larger doesn't mean me. It means the people I bite." And he wriggled away.

(But do not worry too much about Coyote. His brashness and bragging get him killed in more stories than one. Since he is as magical as he is maddening, he always turns up for another adventure. . . .)

COYOTE FLIES WITH THE GEESE

Lipan Apache

Coyote loved to travel. He liked to see new places, find new fruits to taste, hunt new kinds of mice to eat, and try out his tricks on the new people he met. Once, in the fall of the year, he found himself in the north country when the first sharp winds began to blow. He shivered inside his fur coat and said to himself, "Coyote, you should spend this winter lying in the sun!"

So he set out to find the Wild-Geese People.

The Wild-Geese People lived far to the north, so to find them, Coyote had to set his teeth and travel into the cold, wet wind. He passed one camp where people were taking down tipis for a journey south, but he shook his cold, wet paws and kept on. At last he reached the Far North and the camp of the Wild-Geese People. They were taking down their tipis, too. Coyote greeted them.

"I see," he said, "that you will soon be flying to some warm, sunny country for the winter. Do you ever take friends with you? I would like to come with you if I could."

The Wild-Geese People were surprised. They had never heard of such a thing as a coyote flying south. They talked among themselves, and then told Coyote that he was welcome to come along.

"But we must first make wings for you," they said, and they made a pair of wings out of animal skins with the hair scraped off. Then they pasted white feathers all over them so that they looked like real wings. "Now you must try them," they said.

For his first try, Coyote jumped off a high rock and flew around just above the ground. On his second flight he flew a little higher. On his third and fourth tries, he did better and better. The Wild-Geese People shook their heads in surprise.

"You are a *very* good flier—for a coyote," they said. "But we have one more test. You must fly with us."

All of the Wild-Geese People took off, and flew high into the sky. Coyote flew just as high. Next, the geese flew around in a circle, and then did swoops and turns. Coyote circled and swooped and turned, following the leader just as the wild geese did. Back on the ground, the chief of the Wild-Geese People told Coyote that he had done very well.

"We still think you are crazy, but now we know that you can safely join us on our long journey. We will set out tomorrow. But, friend Coyote, one thing you must always remember: On a long journey we always look ahead, never down. If you look down, you will fall out of the sky and smash into the earth. Never, never look down."

Coyote was uneasy. "But I am new at flying. What shall I do if I forget?"

"Then," Chief Wild Goose answered, "when you begin to fall, you must call out, 'My parfleche!' If you say it in time, you will fall softly, and not smash."

The journey was long—very long—for it took them all the way from the Far North to the Far South. They flew across the sky in a flock shaped like an arrow. The chief flew at the point of the arrow. Coyote was always last. As they flew, sometimes they passed over camps. The people looked up, and when they saw Coyote in the distance, they cried out, "Look! Up in the sky! Coyote is coming!" Then everyone looked, and they laughed. "Hai, friend Coyote up there! Throw us a bone! Throw us something good to eat!"

Coyote had to grit his teeth to keep from looking down. He wanted to look down and shout back at them, but he did not. The journey was hard work. Once, when the Wild-Geese People camped beside a great, wide water, Coyote found pretty shells on the shore and strung them together. "They ought to be good for something," he thought. For the rest of the time until they came to the summer camp of the

Wild-Geese People, there was time for nothing but flying, eating, and sleeping.

They stayed at the summer camp in the South Country through the winter months. After a while, with no one but geese to talk to, Coyote began to feel lonely and bored. Every day was the same: sunshine and honking geese, honking geese and sunshine. Every day he sighed and said to himself, "How long must we stay here? How soon are we to fly north?"

At long last, the geese said they were ready to fly home. Coyote flapped along happily at the tail of the V as the flock flew north. Beyond the wide water, the earth below began to look more and more like home, but Coyote kept his eyes only on the geese ahead. "Do not look down. Do not look down," he repeated to himself as he flew.

The nearer they came to their home, the later in the evening the Wild-Geese People flew on. One evening, as they circled in the gloom before gliding down to land on a lake, a glimmer of light far below caught Coyote's eye. A campfire! People who sang songs and ate meat, and did not honk or quack!

He forgot. And looked down.

And fell.

What was the word? If he fell, he was to say a word. Two words. The earth was rushing up at him, and—

"My parfleche!" he howled in fright.

And down he fell.

But he landed as softly as milkweed fluff.

"Aho!" he gasped as he scrambled to his feet and tore off his feathers and wings. "That's the last time *I'll* fly south for the winter!"

COYOTE FREES THE BUFFALO

Kitsai

Coyote and his family lived for a long time in a village near the plains that were his hunting grounds. The hunting was good, for there were many buffalo, but one summer, suddenly, there were none. Coyote and the other hunters traveled for many miles, and found not a one. Everyone in the village grew thin with hunger. Coyote's children cried because their bellies were empty.

"The buffalo are somewhere," Coyote said to himself. "They have not walked up into the sky." So the next morning, and the morning after that, and the morning after *that,* he went out looking. "Somewhere I shall find the buffalo," he told himself each morning. "Why is it that I cannot?"

One day he did not go out onto the plains, but into the woods. Deep in the woods he climbed to the top of a knoll. A wind was blowing there, and in the wind Coyote smelled meat. He stood still and sniffed again. Yes, meat! Buffalo meat! Coyote lifted his nose and followed the smell. He followed it for miles, up and down, across creeks, and through brambles and brush. The smell grew stronger and stronger until he came at last to a lodge that stood by itself at the edge of a wood. Beyond the wood a high bluff rose above the trees. Coyote's nose told him that the meat was nearby, but it told him, too, that this was a bad place, so he hid in the bushes and watched. Soon he saw a small child come out of the lodge to play. The child ran all around the lodge. He threw stones at a tree. At last, he went to sit in the doorway of the lodge and dig in the earth with a stick.

Coyote grinned, and turned himself into a small, fat puppy. His coat was brown and black and silky. His ears and nose were soft. But he forgot to change his whiskers and his eyes. He gave a little yipping bark, and tumbled out of his hiding place.

The little boy looked up and saw him. "Puppy!" he cried. "Puppy come!" And he ran toward Coyote-Pup and took him up in his arms. "Father!" he cried as he ran into the lodge. "Father, look! I found a puppy!"

Crow, who was his father, looked at Coyote-Pup and frowned. "That is not a pup. Something is different about it. Something wrong."

"No! It *is* a puppy!" The child held Coyote-Pup closer.

"No, it is something different, not a real pup," Crow said. "It will be dark soon. Take it out and put it where you found it."

"I will not! It is my puppy. I want to keep it!"

His father frowned. "You cannot. Take it out."

"I won't!"

"Hoh! You will not? Well then, bring it here. We will see whether it is a pup or not," Crow said. He held Coyote-Pup out toward the cook fire and, as it came close to the flames, the pup gave a yip, and wriggled, and made water into the fire.

"Ha!" Crow laughed. "It *is* a pup! Take him. Give him some meat to eat."

So the child did, and Coyote-Pup ate it all up and begged for more. Later, after dark, when the fire had burned down to coals, Crow and his son went to their beds, and Coyote-Pup curled up beside the fire. The others soon fell asleep, but Coyote listened, and only pretended to sleep. When it was safe, he turned back into his own shape, slipped out the door, and followed his nose into the night.

His nose led him through the moonlight to the bluff behind the trees behind the lodge. The bluff looked like solid rock, but Coyote's nose told him that there was an opening. He sniffed and sniffed until he came to a crack. He followed the crack. A door. There *was* a door. He pushed, but it was closed fast. He could find no handle to pull. "Poh!" he said. "Open yourself!"

And the door opened itself.

"Ee-ow!" Coyote yelped and jumped out of the way just in time. A big bull buffalo charged out through the door, and after him thundered cows and bulls and calves, herds of them, enough buffalo to people all of the plains. Coyote danced up and down and urged, "Go, go, go!" as they passed. When the last of the buffalo had run out, Coyote pushed the door shut and hurried after them as they spread out and away toward the plains.

Inside the lodge, Crow woke and heard the thunder of hooves. "Buffalo going by," he thought sleepily. "It is good that all mine are shut up." But he was uneasy, and he rose to go out and make sure. When he came to the rocky bluff, he opened the rock door, saw that the caverns were empty, and shouted out to his son, "They are all gone! I *knew* that pup was no pup!"

When Coyote reached his own village, he called out, "Hoh, everyone! I, Coyote, have brought buffalo for our hunters to hunt. Take up your bows and arrows, and go after them!"

They did, and soon there was meat enough for everyone, and no one went hungry. Because the return of the buffalo had saved the village from starving, the people treated Coyote almost like a chief. If he had not been so pleased with himself that he went around singing of his own great deeds until they grew tired of hearing him, they might even have *made* him chief.

THE GREAT MEATBALL

Comanche

One day a great ball of pounded meat came bobbing along the path that ran from there to here. When he wished to hurry a little, he rolled, but the sky was bright and the buffalo clover blue, so he bobbed along with a cheerful bounce or two. He followed the path a little way into a large blackthorn thicket. Then, puzzled, he stopped and peered ahead.

"Hoh! Is that a coyote lying beside the path through this blackthorn thicket?" the big meatball asked himself. He was too shortsighted to be sure.

"Is that a coyote lying beside the path through this blackthorn thicket?" he called out loud.

Coyote lifted his head a little and answered in a small, weak voice, "It is, but . . . I will soon . . . be dead of hunger. Soon the beetles . . . will gnaw on my bones."

"Hoh, no, Friend!" the meatball exclaimed. He rolled closer and shut his eyes. "Come, take one big bite of me."

So Coyote raised his head and took a big bite.

"Ah-hoh, I feel much better," he said, and sat up. "I will rest here a moment, and then go home."

So the great meatball left him and went on his way.

As soon as the meatball was out of sight, Coyote sprang up and dashed into the thicket. He circled around swiftly, and came out on the trail ahead of the great meatball. Just in time, he dropped to the ground with his eyes shut and his tongue lolling out and his coat all snagged by the thorns. The meatball came rolling along the path through the thicket, and stopped.

"Hoh!" The meatball squinted to see, and said to himself, "Is that another coyote lying beside the path ahead?"

Coyote lifted his head a little. "It is," he croaked faintly. "But not for long. I will soon be dead of hunger, and crows will pick at my bones."

"No, no, poor fellow," said Meatball. "Come, take one big bite out of me."

So Coyote lifted up his head and took a large bite, and swallowed it. "Now, that is much better," he said after a moment. "If I rest me a little, soon I can go on my way."

So the great meatball left him and went on his own way.

Once again, as soon as the meatball was out of sight, Coyote jumped up. He dashed through the thicket, splashed through a stream, and cut back to the trail. Just in time, he threw himself, panting, draggled, and wet, on the ground beside it.

When Meatball came rolling along, he spied a shape stretched out beside the path. "Surely that is yet another coyote," he said to himself, "and each one worse off than the last." Aloud, he called, "Is that a coyote lying there?"

"It is," Coyote gasped. He did not raise his head, but said, "Farewell. I am dying of hunger. Soon the ants will come to polish my bones."

"No, no." Meatball sighed and shut his eyes. "Come, take one big bite of me."

"Very well," Coyote said in a shaky voice. He lifted his head and took a great bite. "I thank you, friend," he said when he had swallowed it. "I feel much better already. I will rest here awhile before I set out."

So Meatball rolled away along the path. He had gone no more than half a mile when, there, at the side of the path ahead, lay a shape very much like a coyote. "Is that a coyote lying there?" he called out.

Coyote's tail gave a weak twitch. "It is," he quavered. "Ah, friend Meatball, I die of hunger. . . ."

The great meatball took a deep breath and said, "Then come, take one big bite of me."

Coyote lifted up his head and opened his mouth wide, but this time the great meatball's eyes were open. He looked, and he saw that Coyote had meat between his teeth.

"You! You ran ahead! It was you every time!" Meatball roared, and he rolled at him. Coyote was faster. He sprang up and ran off as fast as his four legs could carry him. The great meatball rolled after him for miles, but never caught him.

THE FIGHT BETWEEN THE ANIMALS AND INSECTS

Lipan Apache

One fine day Mountain Lion went out for a stroll. He was hungry, but not too hungry. He was happy to pad along, enjoying the warm sunshine and the smell of summer grass in the clearing ahead. He did not see Locust sleeping in the shade under a young redbud tree, and he stepped on him.

"Ai-eeow! Hai, you, Fatfoot! Yes, you, Whisker-face! Who do you think you are, Chief of the World, to come stepping on me?"

"Poh!" scoffed Mountain Lion. "Compared with you, I *am* Chief of the World. Out of my way and let me pass!"

"Why should I? Fatfoot!"

Mountain Lion grinned. "Because my foot *is* fat, Fleabrain."

"Hairy puffball!"

"Bigmouth bug!"

The name-calling went on until both grew so angry that shouting was not enough.

"Stop right there," Locust bellowed. "I am too small to fight you one-to-one, but if you will choose a team from your people, I will choose one from mine. We can hold the match on the flat fields down below."

"Agreed," Mountain Lion growled, and he went off to gather all of the animal people to fight on his side. Everyone agreed to come, from Mouse and Gopher to Buffalo and Bear. All of the insects flocked to join Locust, from the Ant People and all of the other biters, to the Bumblebee People, the Wasps, and all of the other stingers.

Coyote came down to the flats with Mountain Lion at the head of the animal fighters. All they found was the large field and the thick bushes beyond. Locust and his side were nowhere in sight. Coyote said to Mountain Lion, "I think it would be a good idea if I scout around and see where they are, and how many."

So he did. He crept through the brush that bordered the field all around, and when he came near Locust's side, he saw that the bushes there were covered with insects. Crawlers and fliers of every kind were so crowded together that the branches sagged with their weight.

"Where are they, and how many?" Mountain Lion asked when Coyote returned.

"In the bushes, and too many to count," said Coyote.

"So are we," was Mountain Lion's proud reply.

He looked around at the great army of animals. Every family and clan and herd was there, and ready to fight.

"Let's go!" muttered Bear, who thought of himself as the bravest.

"Let's go!" the other animals echoed.

Bear took the lead. The great horde followed him. They moved forward quietly until they reached the middle of the field. Then they charged. The insects charged, too. At once, the animals began to bark and squeak and roar and howl. They rolled on the ground. From Mouse and Gopher to Bear and Buffalo, they whimpered and squealed. The insects crawled into their fur, and bit and stung them again and again. The animals rolled, and jumped up and down, and rubbed up against the bushes, but could not be rid of their enemies. They crawled over one another to reach their own side of the field. Many nearly died.

Not tricky Coyote. He waited while the others moved forward. When the fight started and he heard the first howl, he turned and ran.

HOW RABBIT STOLE
MOUNTAIN LION'S TEETH

Caddo

Rabbit lived with his grandmother. One day when his grandmother had gone out and left him at home alone, he decided that he would go out for a stroll. He wandered here and there and up and down, seeing what there was to see. When he had gone as far as he felt like going, he found himself outside the entrance to Mountain Lion's den. Rabbit could tell by one sniff that Mountain Lion was not at home.

"I should not go in," Rabbit thought. "What if he came home and found me there?"

But Rabbit was too curious to pass without a peek inside. He stuck his nose in, and followed it. Once in, he peered into baskets and peeped into corners. Then, on a rock beside Mountain Lion's bed, he saw Mountain Lion's teeth.

"Hoh-*hoh*!" Rabbit hopped up and down in delight. The very teeth that made everyone so afraid of Mountain Lion! He snatched them up, and ran away home. When he reached his grandmother's burrow, he found that she had returned.

"Oh, Grandmother, see what I have found! Mountain Lion's sharp teeth!" he cried.

But when they had laughed, and danced a little stomp dance, Rabbit frowned. "Grandmother, when Mountain Lion goes home and finds his teeth gone, he will come after them. He will smell my scent and follow it here. We must think of a way to fool him, or he will make us his dinner."

He sat, and thought, and at last he said, "We will build a cook fire just outside the door to the burrow, and put a pot of water on it to boil—your largest pot. Then you must put some nice, round stones in to boil. When Mountain Lion comes looking for his teeth, you must stir the stones in the pot. He will ask 'Why are you cooking these stones?' You must say, 'My grandson, Rabbit, has a very important guest inside. His guest is going to eat them for his dinner.' I will be talking to myself as though I were myself and a friend. Mountain Lion is sure to ask who my friend is."

"And how must I answer him?" Grandmother asked.

"You must say, 'Chief-of-All-the-Beasts,'" Rabbit answered.

So they made a big cook fire, and filled the biggest cook pot with water. When it began to steam, Grandmother put in the good, round stones. Just as the stones came to a boil, Mountain Lion came crashing through the bushes. He rushed straight up to Rabbit's grandmother.

"Rabbit!" he roared. "Where is he? Is he here?"

Inside the burrow, Rabbit began to talk to himself, first in his own voice, and then in a deep, rough one.

"My grandson is inside, talking to his great friend," said Grandmother. She found it hard not to laugh at Mountain Lion without his teeth.

Mountain Lion looked into the cook pot and scowled. "Stones? What are you boiling those stones for, old rabbit?"

"My grandson's fine guest is going to eat them for his dinner," she said with a shrug.

Mountain Lion frowned. "And who is his fine friend?"

"He is Chief-of-All-the-Beasts," Grandmother answered as she stirred the stones.

"Oh," said Mountain Lion. He backed off a little. "Yes, I know him," he said with a weak, bare-gummed grin. Then he whirled around and raced away as fast as his feet would fly.

Rabbit and his grandmother held their breath until he was out of sight, and then laughed until they were too weak to stand.

FOX AND POSSUM

Kitkehahki, South Band Pawnee

Possum had lived for a long while in his hollow tree. He knew every place round about where there were tasty roots, where pecan trees grew, and persimmon trees, too. Like the other animals that wear fur coats, every year when cold weather came and the leaves began to turn yellow, he went out to gather fruit and nuts. When his pouch was full, he traveled home again to store his harvest for the winter. Possum was better at gathering than the other animal people, for he took care not to be followed to his gathering places. He waited until darkness before starting out for the persimmon trees. He took great care to watch behind him on the way. When he came there, he ate the sweet, soft fruit until his belly was full, and then filled the pouch at his belt. Nothing was so good as a ripe persimmon!

One night as he waddled home, Possum met Fox.

At first they stood in the middle of the path and did no more than look at each other. Possum was too frightened to move. It was too late to curl up and pretend to be dead. Then Fox stepped close.

"I am glad to see you, friend Possum," he said with a smile. He reached out to stroke Possum's back, and patted his rump. "Oh, nice and fat. You would taste *so* good!"

Possum was more frightened than before, so frightened that he grew foolish. He stepped around Fox, and walked on. Almost at once, he stopped in horror. He had turned his back on a hungry fox! He whirled to face him again, and found Fox so close that they were almost nose to nose.

Nose.

Without a word, Possum raised a paw to Fox's nose for Fox to smell.

"Aho! You have been eating persimmons!" Fox exclaimed. There was nothing Fox loved better than persimmons. "Ai!" he thought. "What shall I do? If I have Possum for my dinner, I will never know where the persimmon trees are. Perhaps I should eat him for dinner some other time." At last he asked, "When did you pick them?"

"Just now," Possum said quickly. "B-big patch of persimmon trees. Just now."

Fox grinned happily and rubbed his paws. "Just now? Hoh! Take me there!"

"Yes. Oh, yes, yes, of course," Possum said quickly. "Yes, yes, right away!"

So they went, hurrying together, side by side. A cold wind pushed at them, but Possum was shivering so much from fear that he did not notice. When they reached the persimmon trees, Fox stood under the largest and peered upward into the darkness.

"I can smell them," he said. "What are you waiting for? Climb up and pick!"

Possum scrambled up into the branches as fast as his short legs and sharp claws would take him, and perched in a fork of the tree. "At least I will be out of danger up here," he thought unhappily. "For a while." He reached out carefully for a persimmon, and dropped it into Fox's outstretched paws.

"Um-mummm!" Fox licked his lips. "Another, another!"

Possum dropped another.

"Faster, faster!" Fox cried. "You are too slow! Must I come up there to help you?" He frowned, thought for a moment, and then called out, "Come down and help me climb up."

"Yes, yes," Possum answered. "I am coming."

Fox was not a tree climber, but he could reach his front legs far enough around the trunk to raise himself a little. Possum helped by boosting from below. When at last Fox was sitting in the fork of the tree, picking and eating persimmons, Possum crept away through the darkness. The wind had grown much sharper and colder, but as he trotted on home he did not notice. "I'm safe, I'm safe, I'm

safe!" he thought. "And I still have my pouch full of persimmons!"

The next morning the ground was covered with snow and the air was bitterly cold. "I'll just have a look," he thought, and he made his way back to the persimmon trees.

Fox was hanging in the fork of the tree, frozen stiff. Possum sighed, and was sorry. "But if I had not helped him up the tree, that might be me."

SENDEH SINGS TO THE PRAIRIE DOGS

Kiowa

Sendeh the Trickster was always going somewhere, always up to something. "Ai, I am hungry!" he thought one day as he was jogging along and saw a prairie dog village ahead. "I do like roast prairie dog," he said to himself. "But how am I to get enough of them to make a good meal? Shoot one or club one, and all of the others run down their burrows."

Now, Sendeh loved schemes, and because he was clever and cunning, he knew right away what to do. The prairie dogs sat up straight by the holes that were the doors to their burrows and watched him come. They were ready to vanish at his first sudden move.

"Ahoh, my friends!" Sendeh called out. "How handsome and happy you look this morning! It is a long while since I have seen such a bright-eyed and beautiful company of dancers."

The prairie dogs all pricked their ears up, for they loved more than anything else to dance. One beat from a distant drum or one note from a faraway flute, and prairie dogs would jump up and dance the day and half the night away.

"We were not dancing," said one. "We have no drummer."

"No drummer?" exclaimed Sendeh. "Why, then, I shall be your drummer. Come over here where the ground is clear for dancing, and I will beat time on the ground with my stick. Make room," he said as the prairie dogs crowded around. "Make room for me to beat time. Now dance! And close your eyes to hear the beat better while I sing."

Some of the little prairie dogs closed their eyes, and they all began to dance. Sendeh began to sing, "*Tsako, tsetsu' tsetsu' to! Batontote owiya! Owiya palotsi!*"

> *Prairie dog, prairie, prairie,*
> *Tail, shake tail as I sing!*
> *As I sing, I beat the ground!*

"Wonderful!" Sendeh called out after they had danced for a while. "But I grow warm. Let us sit down and rest a little."

The prairie dogs chattered away as they rested, and told Sendeh he was a fine drummer and a fine fellow. When he said, "Come, let us dance again," they leaped up at once and began. They closed their eyes and danced in a happy dream. "*Prairie dog, prairie, prairie . . . ,*" Sendeh sang, and as he sang he beat time with his stick on the dancers. He hit every one of them but one little prairie dog on the far side of the circle who had kept her eyes half open.

The little one squeaked and ran for her burrow, with Sendeh close behind, hitting with his stick but missing each time. "Hoh-hah!" he said as she disappeared down her hole. "Go, then. Someone must be the mother of the prairie dogs to come, so now it will be you."

Feeling pleased with himself, he carried the other prairie dogs down to the riverbank, where he heaped them up, piled on wood, and made a fire. Then he looked around for something to do while he waited for his dinner to roast. Not far away, he saw a tree with branches well set for climbing, and a forked branch that gave him a good idea. "I will practice my magic on that tree. I will sit up in that fork, and tell the branches to twist around me," he said.

Sendeh was not just an ordinary fellow who played tricks. He had learned some magic powers, and always wished for more. What could be more fun than making rocks or water or trees do what he wanted? So he climbed the tree, and perched where the branches forked. "Branches," he commanded, "twist around me so that I cannot get free!" And they did.

Sendeh did not know that Coyote was nearby. Coyote had sniffed the roasting meat, and hurried to investigate. He hid behind a clump of willows and listened. When he saw what Sendeh was doing, he crept away through the trees. A few moments later, Coyote came into sight on the path down to the river. He stumbled along. He held his stomach. He groaned. His face lit up when he saw Sendeh.

"Hoh! Sendeh! It is you! I am starving, and I smell meat in your cook fire! Will you not be a friend, and when you have eaten all the best parts, leave the bones for me?"

"Indeed, I will not," Sendeh called down. "I killed my meat for myself. People should feed themselves. Go away and hunt your own prairie dogs!"

"But I am too weak," Coyote whimpered. "I cannot lift a club or pull a bowstring."

"Pah!" Sendeh shouted down at him. "I keep my food for myself, and I eat bones and all!"

Sendeh was about to say, "Tree, go back to your own shape," but Coyote was quicker. "Tree, stay that way!" he called out. "That Sendeh is a bad one. He is too selfish to spare even a bone. Keep him up there."

Sendeh stroked the tree and spoke softly. "Tree, go back to your own shape."

It did not.

"Tree," Sendeh said more sharply, "go back to your own shape!"

It would not.

"Tree! Go back to your own shape!" Sendeh commanded.

The tree still stayed as it was, and Coyote saw that he was safe. He went to the fire, raked off the coals, and began to eat the roast prairie dogs.

"TREE! GO BACK TO YOUR OWN SHAPE!" Sendeh roared. When the tree would not, he began to wheedle. "Come, friend Coyote. Let me come down, and I will give you half."

Coyote did not answer. His mouth was too full. As he ate more and more, Sendeh called out, "You are eating it *all*! You must leave some for me. Hai-ee! If you do not leave some for me, when I get free I will hunt you down!" He was so angry that he drew his knife and stabbed at the tree, but still it would not let him go.

Coyote finished at last, wiped his mouth, moved off a little way, and called back, "Tree, go back to your own shape!" Then he ran.

The tree's branches sprang back to their own shape. Sendeh climbed down and ran to the fire, but he found nothing but clean bones. "If it takes until winter, I will find that coyote," he growled. And he set out to find him. Every coyote he met, he caught.

"Hoh, Nephew! Are you the fellow who ate my prairie dogs?"

"It was not I!" every coyote yelped. "Do not hit me!"

"Then open your mouth," Sendeh commanded. But when he looked inside their mouths, he never saw or smelled any meat sticking in the teeth of any coyote he caught.

He may be looking still.

THE DESERTED CHILDREN

Comanche

Not far from the people's summer camping place was a creek where the children liked to play. Early one day in the season of dry grass and yellow leaves, four children ran through the grass and down through the fringe of black willows to the creek. An older girl came too, bringing corn cakes and carrying her little brother on her back, and all six played together. They jumped from rock to rock. They skipped stones across the water. They tried to catch small fish by tickling their bellies, but frightened them away by laughing too much.

At the same time, in the camp, the people were busy. They rolled blankets into bundles. They packed baskets. They took down their lodges. When everything was packed, they set out for their winter hunting grounds.

The children at the creek played all day. When at last they fell quiet and sat down to rest, one child turned to look back through the willow trees toward the camp. *Where were the lodges?* Their tops had shown above the waving grass. Now the child saw nothing. He ran through the trees and out into the grass and saw that they truly were gone. He ran back to his friends, crying out, "Come! The lodges are gone! Everyone is gone! Come, look!"

The others laughed. "Liar! You cannot trick us!" they said, but they sent another child to look.

The second child came running back. "Ai, come!" she cried. "They *are* gone."

The children, still playing on the bank, laughed. "No, no, you cannot trick us," they said, but the older Sister herself went to look. When she, too, called back, "They *are* gone! Come, all of you," they knew it was true.

Sister took Little Brother up on her back, and led the way. When they reached the camp, the sun had already set, but they found the trail the people had left. They set out to follow it, and the deeper the dusk grew, the more they hurried. In a little while they met Coyote coming the other way.

"Take care," Coyote warned after he heard their tale. "Big Owl lives beside the trail, across the creek not far from here. You must be more quiet than mice when you pass, or he will hear you."

Big Owl! The children shivered as they hurried on. The shadows were deep in the woods. Soon after they came to the place where the trail crossed a creek, they saw the dark shape of a lodge among the trees. Little Brother began to cry.

"Hush!" Sister warned in a whisper. But he did not.

"*Who-oo, who is passing my lodge?*" a voice called.

"Hai! I hear my nephew crying. He wants to come to his uncle. Come, come, bring my nephew to me."

"Uncle!" Little Brother cried. "I want to go to Uncle!"

Sister and the other children did not stop. "That is not Uncle," she whispered. "Coyote told us. It is Big Owl."

"No!" Little Brother began to cry. "Uncle! I want to go to Uncle."

"Coyote tells lies," one child said.

"Coyote plays tricks," said another.

Sister nodded. Coyote did play tricks. He *did*. Slowly she turned and led the children toward the lodge, but she was still afraid. "It is Big Owl, not our uncle. He will eat us all," she thought, and she began to plan how they might escape.

As soon as the children came near the door of the lodge, out hopped Big Owl with his great round eyes, sharp curved beak, and feathers sticking up like a cat's ears. He was *very* big, too big ever to fly.

"Whoo-who!" he hooted. "Whoo-oo—who shall I eat first for my dinner?"

The younger children began to cry, but Sister spoke up bravely. "Any of us will do. We are all very tender, but we are all very dirty. We should first go down to the creek to wash."

Big Owl stared with his round yellow eyes, but said, "Very well, wash. But hurry back."

Down by the creek the children met a frog.

"Oh, Frog!" cried Sister. "Big Owl wants to eat us. Can you help us?"

"I will if I can," Frog said.

"You can if you will," said Sister. "We will run off, and when Big Owl calls, you must answer for us. Say, 'No, we are still washing.' If you can fool him long enough, we will be far away before he knows we are gone."

"I will," Frog said happily, for he did not like Big Owl.

Soon after the children ran off, Big Owl shouted out, "Little girls, little boys, I want my dinner. Come back!"

"We are still washing," Frog called in a high voice.

After a little while Big Owl called again, and Frog answered again. "Wait, we are still washing!" Every time Big Owl called, Frog answered, "Wait, wait, we are still washing."

Big Owl grew impatient, and at last he knew that the children must be gone. He sprang down the path to the creek, carrying all of his weapons. "Hoo, hoo-oo, hoo-hoo?" he hooted, and then he saw Frog. "*You?*"

Frog jumped up and down. "Hoh! I tricked you! The children are gone, gone!"

"You long-legged rascal! You let my dinner escape!"

Big Owl struck at Frog with his stick, but Frog only gave a laugh and jumped into the creek.

Angry and hungry, Big Owl started out after the children. He could see in the dark almost as well as at dusk. Before long he saw the children far ahead. He waved his big stone club and bounded along even faster.

The children had come to a creek too wide and swift to cross. In the moonlight, Sister saw Fish Crane sitting on the bank and cried out to him, "Oh, Crane! Big Owl is chasing us! He wants to eat us. Will you help us?"

"*Tuk-tuk,* I will if I can," Fish Crane said.

"You can if you will," said Sister.

So Fish Crane took a louse from the red feathers atop his head and gave it to Sister. "Put this in your mouth," he said. "It tastes bad, but do not spit it out until all of you reach the other side. If you do this, I will stretch my leg over the creek for a bridge so that you may walk across."

Sister agreed. She put the louse in her mouth, took her little brother up on her back again, and led the children across. Then she spat out the louse, and they ran on.

Big Owl came to the creek in time to see them run. "Hoh, Crane," he cried. "There goes my dinner! Help me across the creek so that I may catch them."

"Only if you do as I say," said Fish Crane, and he made him the same offer he had made Sister.

"Give me the louse," Big Owl snapped. But it tasted so bad that he spat it out in the middle of the stream, and fell off Fish Crane's long leg into the water. When at last he reached the far bank, he shook the water from his feathers and hurried on.

Before long, he spied the children out on the moonlit open prairie. Far ahead, they looked back and saw him, too.

"Oh, oh! What shall we do?" they all cried.

A little way ahead of them, a buffalo calf lay asleep in the grass. "Hoh, Buffalo Calf!" Big Sister called out. "Big Owl is chasing us. If you do not help us, he will eat us up!"

"I will if I can," said Buffalo Calf, and he stood up. "Stand behind me." And when Big Owl came up, Buffalo Calf put his head down and gave a brave snort.

Big Owl swung his great wooden hammer in the air. "Foolish Calf, you cannot frighten me. If you do not give me my dinner, I will smash you with my hammer."

Buffalo Calf stood still and pawed the ground. When Big Owl raised his hammer, Buffalo Calf ran at him, and hit him, and threw him straight up to the moon.

When the children had thanked him, they ran

on until morning. They came at last to the camp where their people had stopped for the night. There, they found their parents, who had not discovered that the children were missing until they made camp for the night. And all was well.

And now, when the moon is full, you can see Big Owl still sitting on the moon with his hammer.

Mountain Lion and the Four Sisters

Osage

Long ago, in the early days of the world, four sisters lived together in a grass lodge at the edge of the hill country. They had lived on their own since their parents died. The oldest sister cooked their meals. The next-to-oldest wove grass mats for the floor of their lodge, and to trade with people in the summer camp nearby. The next-to-youngest wove small mats on which to serve food, both to use and to trade. The youngest girl picked berries for cooking and grass for weaving, and flowers to braid in her hair.

One day Sister Cook and Littlest Sister went out with a gourd pot to bring water, and found a dead skunk. "If only you were good meat." Sister Cook sighed, for their only foods were roots and berries and greens. When they went out the next day the skunk was gone, but they saw a dead raccoon. "If only I had not had a little raccoon for a pet long ago," Sister Cook said, "I would take you home for food. But I cannot." On the day after that they went out and found the raccoon gone, but as they dug for sweet roots Sister Cook shaded her eyes and said, "I see something the size of a doe." They went to look and found a dead deer.

"Ah, hai, see what some hunter has left today!" exclaimed Sister Cook. "And it is fresh!"

Littlest Sister clapped her hands. "Venison!"

"I will butcher it," Sister Cook said, and she did, and they carried the meat home to their lodge. There they cooked tender venison strips for their dinner, and sliced the rest thin and strung it up to dry and keep.

But the next day, when Sister Cook went out with her gourds to bring water, she saw Mountain Lion trotting away through the trees with a turkey in his mouth. As soon as he was gone, she ran back to the lodge.

"Sisters!" she cried. "We must run! I have seen Mountain Lion among the trees close by. He must be the hunter who killed our deer. He will eat us for eating it! We must leave this place and find a new home far from here."

The sisters gathered up food for the journey, and a few belongings. They put the deer's antlers—which were all that was left of it—in the fire. Then they ran, and just in time. A little while later, Mountain Lion crept up to their camp, peered into the lodge, and saw that they were gone. He sniffed at the ground to find their trail. "*Arr-rrh!*" he growled to himself. "I should have had them for dinner long ago."

He found the path the girls had taken, and padded off after them. Suddenly, in the lodge behind him, the deer antlers sang out, "Where are you off to, you greedy girl-eater?"

Mountain Lion whirled and hurried back. He looked in the grass lodge and everywhere around, but no one was there. He started out again at a run, angrier than before. When he saw the girls far ahead, he gave a loud growl and ran faster. The oldest sister stopped when she heard him, and stamped her foot on the ground. Where she stamped, an apple tree sprang up, and its apples fell to the ground.

Mountain Lion stopped, and sniffed. The apples were so fat and red, and smelled so sweet that he had to take a bite. He bit, then ate one, then another, and another, and another. When he set out again, the girls were far ahead, but before long they heard his grumbling growl on the path behind them. Next-to-Oldest Sister stopped when she heard it, and stamped her foot on the ground as her sister had. This time, a pawpaw tree sprang up, and pawpaws dropped down. Mountain Lion could not pass by the soft, sweet pawpaws. He stopped, and ate. And ate. When Mountain Lion started off again, the girls were farther ahead than before, but they were very tired. He came up fast behind them.

Next-to-Youngest Sister heard Mountain Lion's snarly snort and stopped and stamped her foot.

Where she stamped, a deep, wide ravine opened up. When Mountain Lion came to its edge, he could not cross it. The girls sat resting on the other side.

Crafty Mountain Lion called out in a voice as sweet as honey. "Clever girls!" he cried. "How did you cross a gap too wide for as great a leaper as I?"

"On this!" Littlest Sister piped up, and she picked up a stick. "We put it down and stretched it out, and walked across it."

"Ai! Wonderful! May I try?"

Littlest Sister put the stick down at the edge of the ravine, and it stretched itself out until it touched the other side. Mountain Lion looked at the stick, tapped it with a paw, and then stepped onto it and crept out over the ravine. When he reached the middle, the stick broke, and he fell.

The four sisters leaned out to peer over the edge. All they saw below was swift, deep water. Live or dead, Mountain Lion had been swept downstream and away.

So the girls headed home to another tasty dinner of his venison.

How Poor Boy
Won His Wife

Kiowa-Apache

Poor Boy had no family. None of the Apaches of his tribe cared for him, though some gave him food. He had no weapon, so hunting was hard. Sometimes he fished in the creek. Sometimes he went out at night to set snares for jackrabbits. One night, out on a hill not far from the camp, he heard the sound of weeping.

He crept around to the shadow side of the hill, and upward. On top of the hill, a girl sat in the moonlight, weeping for her brother, who had been killed far away, in a fight with Comanches.

"Ai, ai!" the girl mourned. "I miss him so! Our parents cannot even say a blessing over his bones. If I could only see his bones! If only some brave were to bring me one of his bones, even the smallest of his little-finger bones, I would . . . I would marry him!"

"What did you say?" asked a voice.

The girl turned and saw Poor Boy standing not far away. She spoke through her tears. "I said that if any brave brings me even one of my brother's bones, I will marry him."

"Then I am going to find your brother's bones and bring them home," Poor Boy said quietly. "Come stand on this spot on this hill each day and watch to the northeast, toward the Comanche country. Keep watch, for I will return."

Then Poor Boy went down the hill to a place where he could be alone, and pray. At dawn, in his mind, his spirit spoke to him. "Do you see that great dust in the distance?" it said. "It is from the hooves of the horses of the Comanche. There is where you will find her brother."

So Poor Boy journeyed to the Comanche country. When he came there, the Comanches were holding a Sun Dance. All day, Poor Boy sat behind a tree on a hill a long way off, and watched. As he watched, his spirit spoke to him again. "You will find Brother at the center of the lodge at the center of the camp," it said. But too many people were there. Many were dancing. Many more watched the dancing. "I will wait until night, and creep close then," thought Poor Boy.

After dark, he crept down to the open-sided lodge that was the dancing shelter. Some people were still there, so he sat in the shadows and listened. As he listened, he seemed to hear a long sigh overhead, and a voice that whispered, *"Hoh, I am tired, so tired."* Poor Boy looked up at the fork of the center pole. He saw a young man tied there hand and foot. It was the girl's brother, and he was alive!

Poor Boy sat looking up and trying to think of a plan. Even if he could climb so high, he would be seen, and caught.

"If only," he wished, "someone here had a kind heart and would help me help him!"

"Very well," a tiny voice answered. "*I* will help."

Poor Boy looked down and saw a spider sitting beside him.

"I will help," the spider said. "Climb this pole, and I will follow."

Poor Boy was about to say, "I cannot—they will see me," when he looked down and saw that he himself had become a spider. At once he raced up the nearest pole as fast as his eight legs would take him. From the top, he ran along a crossbeam to the center pole. Spider followed close behind.

"I am so tired," the girl's brother whispered. "I am so tired."

"All is well, Brother-in-Law," Poor Boy piped up in his small spider's voice. "I have come to take you home."

Poor Boy and Spider cut through the cords that bound the young man. To his surprise, when he tried to rub his wrists, he found that he, too, had become a spider. Together, the three spiders raced along the wooden beam to the pole at the outer rim. Before they climbed down, Spider warned the other two that great dangers awaited them.

"The Comanches will chase you, for as soon as your feet touch ground, you will be human beings, not spiders. They will see you, but before they capture you, you must run into the tipi of their chief. The chief and his wife are alone there. His people will gather around the tipi, but they will not enter. The chief will test you, and if you pass his tests, you will have a chance to escape. When you go, the Comanche people will chase you, but they cannot kill you unless you look back. You may stop four times to catch your breath, but do not look back. No matter what you hear behind you, do not look back!"

The two Apache boys did as Spider told them. When they reached the foot of the pole and saw that they had their own hands and feet and selves back, they ran straight to the chief's tipi. The Comanche people shouted and ran after them, but stopped in the doorway. No one followed Poor Boy and the girl's brother inside.

The Comanche chief looked at the two young men. When at last he spoke, he said, "You both are brave, but my people wish to kill you. We will smoke a pipe together, and I will decide what to do." He held out two pipes, one black and one red. "Choose which you will smoke."

Spider had told them, "Be sure to take the black pipe. If you take the red one, they can kill you." So the two young men chose the black, and the people at the doorway muttered angrily.

After the chief had filled and lit the black pipe, each young man took a puff, and then Poor Boy handed it back to the chief. The chief put it aside and offered them next two drinking bowls. One held red water. One held black water. The boys remembered Spider's second warning. "Be sure to take the black drink," he had told them. "If you take the red one, they will kill you." So they took the black water and, between them, drank it down.

"I have decided," the chief said. "You may go." He gave a wave of his hand, and the Comanche people moved back to let them pass.

The young men ran.

As soon as they passed out of the Comanche camp and over the brow of the hill beyond, the people started running after them. They shouted as they ran. The chase went on and on into the night. When the boys had to stop to catch their breath, they could hear the yells of the Comanches as they drew closer. The boys were frightened, but they did not look back. They caught their breath and set off again running. After another hour they had to stop again. This time, the cries of the Comanches sounded close at their backs. The boys trembled, but did not look behind them. They caught their breath, then ran again.

When they stopped to rest the third time, the shouts of the Comanches were so close in their ears that it seemed they would run right over them. The boys jumped up in alarm, but even in their fright they remembered Spider's words, and did not look back as they ran on. When they stopped for the fourth time to rest, they heard nothing but silence.

The remainder of their journey went swiftly. Near dawn they saw that they had come almost to their own camp. In the camp, the girl rose just before daylight and went up onto the hill as she did every morning. When she looked out across the land, she saw the figures of two men coming across the prairie.

"Brother! Oh, my brother!" she shouted as she ran to meet him. She threw her arms about her brother, then led him back to the camp. As they went, she called out to everyone, "It is my brother! My brother is home again!"

"My son, we thought you were dead," cried his father. "How have you come back to us? Who brought you home?"

"This fellow," his son said. He pulled his companion forward.

"Poor Boy? He has brought you?" The old man was surprised, but then he heard of the girl's promise. He saw the cuts on his son's wrists and ankles from the cords. He listened to the boys' tale. "Wife," he said, "prepare a feast for our daughter's husband." And she did. And to every guest who came, the old man told the tale, and he pointed out Poor Boy and proudly called him Son-in-Law.

And that is how Poor Boy won the wife he wanted.

THE GHOST WOMAN

Kiowa–Apache

Once, a chief lost his daughter. The girl fell ill and died. Her father and mother grieved as they buried her, and built a tipi over her grave. Inside the tipi they made their daughter's bed and spread it with soft furs for blankets. They brought her baskets and clothes and ornaments from their own tipi. They built a fire circle at the center of the earth floor, and piled up firewood outside the doorway. When the new tipi was just like their home when she was alive, they left. Then, because autumn was coming, and because he was so sad in that place, the chief took his people and moved to their winter camp far away.

One day some winters later, a raiding party went out from the chief's camp in search of horses. They traveled far into Comanche country, and in the snowy woods one young man strayed too far from his companions, and was lost. When the snow stopped falling, he could not find them or their trail. At last he decided to return home, and turned back.

The way was long and the wind cold, but the young man ran on and on. After he had traveled many miles, snow began to fall again. He thought he saw a tipi not far off, but the blizzard swept

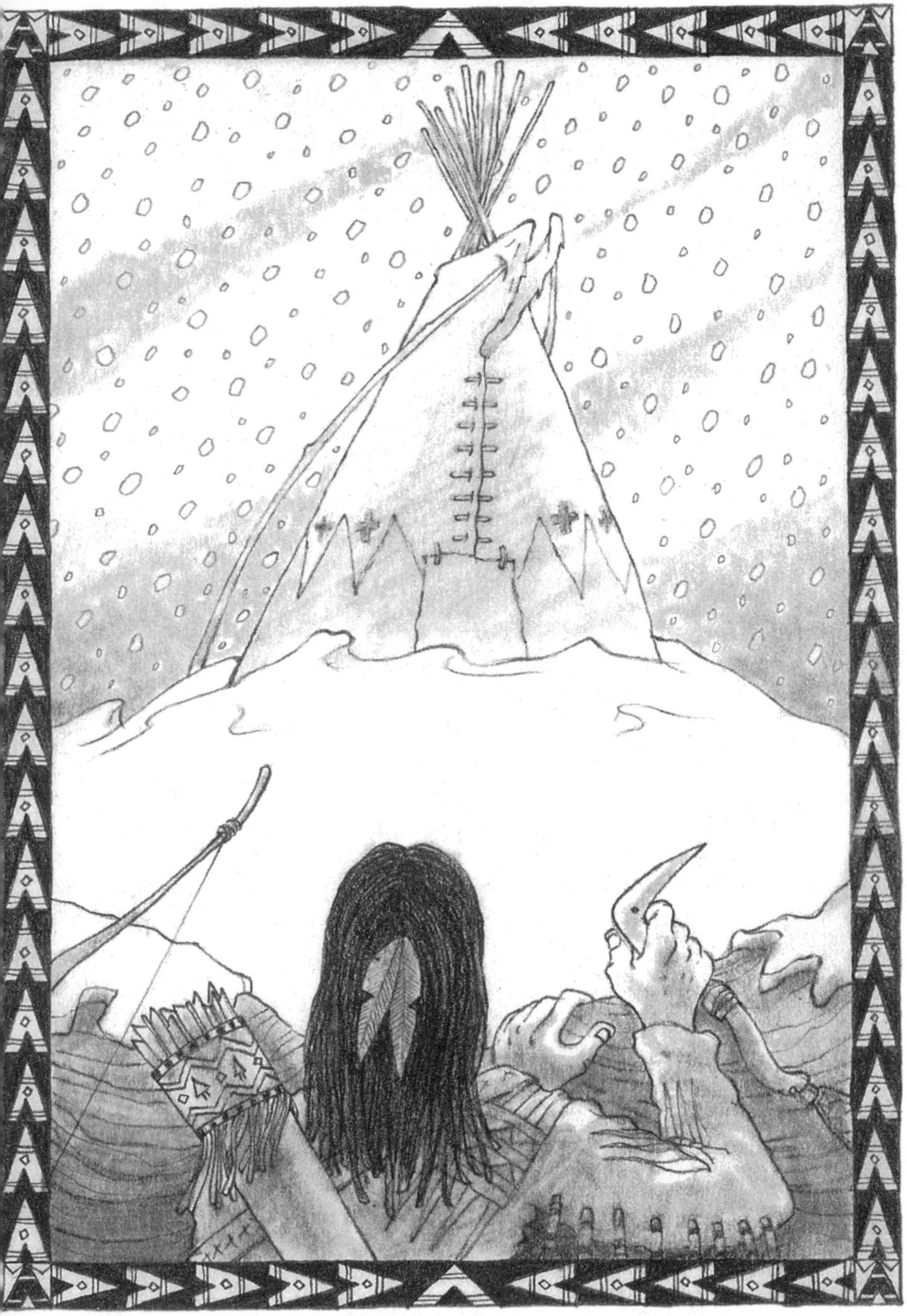

around him, and he was at the tipi's doorway before he recognized it. It was the dead girl's tipi.

"It is bad medicine to enter this place," he said aloud to himself, "but I will die if I do not." So he unfastened the hide covering the opening and stepped in.

The tipi inside was as cold as the blizzard outside. The young man shivered with the cold, but then he remembered the woodpile outside. When he had brought in wood, he took a bit of dry tinder from his pouch, and struck a spark with his flint rock to start the fire. Once the wood was burning, he brought in more, then sat up to watch the flames. Because the girl was buried there, he was afraid to go to sleep.

In the morning the snow still was falling, so the young man brought in more wood. He sat down again to watch the fire. For a little while he watched, but then weariness won. He slipped into sleep where he sat, and fell over beside the fire.

The young man slept for two days. When he awoke, he was covered with a fur robe and someone was shaking him. A voice said, "You have slept long enough. Come, wash your face and hands, and eat."

He lay still, too frightened to open his eyes. Who could it be but the ghost of the chief's daughter? In his terror he pulled the robe over his head and fled back into sleep. When he awoke again, someone was pulling the covers away.

"Come," he heard a young woman's voice say. "Do not be afraid of me."

He opened his eyes and saw that it truly *was* the chief's daughter. She brought food to him, and he ate. As he ate, he stared at her in wonder. How could she be dead when he could see that she was alive?

"Don't think about that," she said.

In his wonder, he did not hear. He could not take his eyes from her face, for she was very beautiful. He wondered whether he could take her home to their people.

"Yes," she said. "I will go with you." And he knew then that she could hear his thoughts.

"I will go with you," she said, "but you must never call me Ghost Woman. If you grow angry with me, you may punish me, but do not call me that."

He was puzzled. "Why should I not?"

"Because if you do, I shall go away and never return."

"No!" he cried, for already he loved her too much to think that he might be parted from her. "What would happen to me?"

"Not long after I was gone, you too would vanish from this land. We would meet again, but far from here."

The young man promised then never to call her a ghost, and at once they set out for their people's winter camp. When at last they saw the tipis in the distance, the young man slowed his pace. "When we come to the camp, what if people recognize you and are afraid? They will ask questions. What shall I say?"

"They must know," the young woman answered. "You must tell them our story."

When the young man and woman came to the camp, everyone gathered around them and stared. They called to others to come. "Is it she?" some whispered. "No, she would be older. It is someone who looks like her," some answered. But the young woman had a small brother who was now half grown. Her brother came to look at her, then hurried back to the chief's tipi.

"Mother!" he cried. "The girl who came with the lost warrior is my sister!"

His mother was frightened. "Never say that, my son. We buried your sister, and grieved for her. She is gone."

But the boy refused to believe her. Time after time he went back to the young man's tipi to look at the young woman, and each time he went home to say, "Mother, she *is* my sister!" At last his mother said to the chief, "Husband, let us go and see for ourselves."

So they went, and looked, and knew that she was their daughter, and welcomed her with tears and happiness. In the years that followed, the young man and woman lived together as husband

and wife, and had a son. The young man loved his small son so much that he worried as he watched him play.

"Wife," he said. "I worry. What if some day, in anger, I forget and call you the name I must not. If you were to go away and I to follow, what would happen to our boy?"

"He would follow us wherever we went," his wife replied.

Summers and winters went by, and the wife grew silent. At last this so angered her husband that he shouted at her. Without thinking, he called her Ghost Woman.

She rose, stepped out of the tipi, and vanished.

A few days later, the husband vanished too, and then the son. Even their tipi disappeared. The people searched for them everywhere, but found no sign of them.

All that was left of them was their story.

THE BOY WHO KILLED THE HILL

Osage

The people traveled for many miles before they found a good place for a camp. They looked for a wide, level place with good grass, near a creek, and with a hill nearby to give a view of the country round about. From atop a good hill they could keep a watch for enemies, and for buffalo and deer and wild horses, too. When they came at last to a place that offered all of that, they stopped, built lodges, hunted and fished, planted corn, and soon had a fine village.

For a while.

After a while the hunters began to notice that there were fewer deer and buffalo and horses. For the first time, the people had days without meat. They grew more frightened when one hunter, and another and another, never came home from the hunt. Dogs vanished too, and even a child or two, and one or two of the warriors who kept watch on the top of the hill. Then one day a hunter came running breathless back to the village. "The hill!" he shouted out. "The hill! I saw it! The hill opened up its mouth and ate the buffalo I shot!"

The people set watchers at a safe distance from the hill to watch, and the watchers saw, and came back to say that the tale was true.

"The hill will eat up everything!" the people cried. "When all of our game is eaten, and all of our hunters, our lodges will be next, and all of us down to the smallest!"

One boy in the village was not afraid. One morning he said to his mother, "I am going to kill that hill."

"No! You must leave it alone!" his mother cried. "It does not eat only buffalo and deer. It eats people!"

"I shall kill it even so," the boy said, and he took his knife from its sheath and began to sharpen it. When its edge was keen enough to slice a stone, he went off to face the hill. He stood at its foot and shouted out, "Hoh, Big Belly! Wake up and eat *me* if you dare! If you can eat warriors and buffalo, why should you fear eating me?"

The hill stirred itself. "Who said that?" it rumbled. "A boy! How dares a boy to speak so to me? If you wish to be eaten, Boy, you shall have your wish." And it opened its mouth and swallowed him whole.

Once the boy was inside, he made his way down the hill's throat. When he reached its heart, he pulled out his knife, reached up, and sliced a deep slit.

"*Unnh-nnh!*" groaned the hill. "Such a small bite of a boy to make me so ill! Ai, ai, ai!" it cried, and little by little it died.

The boy made his way back to the hill's open mouth, and stepped out. "I have really killed it!" he crowed. Then he heard a great sound of hooves and footsteps, and looked inside the hill's mouth again. There he saw a great buffalo trotting toward him, and behind it came every creature the hill had eaten—buffalo, deer, turkeys, dogs, children, and hunters. The wild animals raced away into the woods, and the children and men and dogs ran shouting and barking back to their lodges.

When the first excitement was over, the chief of the village called a council of all the people to decide how they should reward the boy for his great deed. First it was decided to order that a great banquet be prepared, and that the chiefs of all the villages nearby be invited to join the celebration. "That is not enough for such bravery!" the people said, and they agreed at last that what he should have was the chief's beautiful daughter for his wife.

Neither the boy nor the chief's daughter said "No."

WHITE FOX

Kiowa

The people who lived together in the large camp by the river were often hungry. The men spent day after day in hunting, but game was hard to find. The women went out gathering, but after the dry summer, the fruits were small and the berries few.

One man and woman in the camp had a young son of twelve summers old. One day, as the father readied his pack and took up his bow and arrows, the boy begged to go with him.

His mother was frightened. "No, no," she said to his father. "He is too young to go."

"I will be quiet, Father, and not frighten the deer or beaver or jackrabbits," the boy promised. "Please take me."

"No, no," his mother said to his father. "He would be of no use to you."

"I will carry your club, Father," the boy said. "And on the way home I will help carry the meat."

"No! No, let him stay here," his mother cried to his father. "The wind outside is too sharp and the air too cold."

But the father looked at his son and saw that what he wished to share was a hunter's work, not a boy's game. "I will take him with me, Wife," he said.

Some time after the hunter and his son went out from the camp, snow began to fall. Soon they saw buffalo tracks in the snow, and followed them all the morning and past midday. Halfway between midday and sunset, they came up to the little herd, and the hunter shot a good, fat bull.

"Now we will butcher it," the father said. As he worked, he taught his son how to skin the buffalo for its hide, how to divide the joints for roasting, and how to cut from the bones the parts for slicing into strips for drying. By the time they finished, the sun had set.

"This buffalo was very large," the father said. "The two of us cannot carry all of it home. I must go back and bring our pack dogs. You must stay here and guard the meat. We will make a heap of it, and I will cover you and the meat with the buffalo's hide. The fresh meat will keep you warm. You will not be afraid."

"No, Father," the boy said. "I will not be afraid."

So the father put aside some pieces of meat to take to his hungry wife, and covered the rest, and his son, with the buffalo hide. Then he set off for the camp, to bring their dogs.

Because it was far, the journey took a long while. When he came to his lodge, his wife met him at its door.

"Where is our son?" she cried out.

"I have brought you meat, and left him to keep watch over the rest."

"Ai-ee!" she wailed. "You have left him alone in the snow? Such a little boy?"

But the father was not afraid for his son. He gathered his dogs, and set out again.

At that same time of the night, out on the prairie, a wolf out searching for some small animal to eat smelled the buffalo meat, and the boy. When he came to the humped-up buffalo hide, he called out, "Man-child, I am hungry. Will you give me meat?"

"I will," said the little boy from under the buffalo hide. When the wolf heard this, he howled long and loud, and other wolves answered, and came.

"Where is your chief?" the first wolf asked.

"He has been killed, and gone to the sky above," the others answered. "You are as strong as he, so we will take you for our chief."

The first wolf turned to the boy, who peeped out from under the buffalo skin. "I am Guiyaso, Gray Wolf. When I could, I have always killed any creature worth eating, but I will not eat you, because you are willing to feed me and my people. More than that, I will give you the same power that I have. It is the power to see everything, to miss nothing." And he began to sing a wolf song.

When the song was finished, the boy held out a piece of meat. Gray Wolf took it and went a little way away to eat it.

Another wolf came near and said to the boy, "I will give you the power I have. I always have enough to eat. I never go hungry. This same power I give to you."

The boy gave him, too, a piece of meat, and he went off to eat it.

Next came a handsome white wolf, who said to him, "I give you a name, *Alpaguit'aide,* White Fox, and the power to see all that there is in the world, whether you are in your tipi or out under the sky." The boy handed out a piece of meat to him, too.

A moment later, a shout rang out. *"Hai-hai-hai!"* The hunter had returned. From far off he saw the wolves, and was frightened. Wolves! Wolves must have smelled the meat, and eaten boy, meat, and all! As he raised his club and ran toward the place, he thought he saw the buffalo hide move. Then he thought he heard his son's voice. "Aho!" he cried. "My son!"

"Stop, Father!" the boy called. "Stop there until I say 'Come.'"

Three times he called out "Stop!" and "Come!" as his father approached. When his father came near, he saw that the wolves were gone, his son was unharmed, and most of the meat was still there. The boy sat up very straight, and his eyes shone.

"No, Father. You must not touch me," he said.

His father saw then that the difference in him came from some new power. He said quickly, "Do not tell me. You must keep it to yourself. And do not worry about the meat that is gone. It is of no importance. I am only happy to find you safe and well. Your mother wept many tears. She feared that we would never see you again. Come, let us pack up our meat and return to her."

So they did, and at dawn they came into the camp by the river. When she saw them coming, the boy's mother ran to meet them. "My son is safe!" she cried. "Oh, my son, I was sure that bears or wolves had eaten you!" When she saw how much meat they brought, she laughed.

"Now I am hungry!" she said. "I have cooked a stew, but have not swallowed a bite since your father left me. Come, let us go in and eat!"

Afterward, the boy told his new name, White Fox, to his mother and father and the people. The people learned that White Fox could find game when others came home empty-handed, that he always knew when enemies were coming, that in war he could find every enemy camp, and that he could lead a raid and bring home a great prize of horses. For all this, though he was only a boy, they followed wherever he led.

THE TONKAWA
AND THE BEAR

Tonkawa

Five young Tonkawa men, out hunting, were headed north toward the plains. They traveled through the hills, following the streams, camping at dusk for a meal of turkey or rabbits roasted over their fire, and a good night's sleep. In the morning, after a bite to eat, they went on their way again. On the third morning they came out onto the plains.

They had not gone far before one young man called to the others, and pointed. "See there! A buffalo. He follows the track this way. I see no others."

"Let us kill him and eat a real meal!" another said. "If we go back to the hills and hide ourselves, we can surround him when he comes."

"Without a chase!" said a third. The other young men laughed, and were pleased. All five agreed, and they turned and trotted back the way they had come.

They had not gone far when they heard a great roar. They stopped, and drew together, and looked all around. "I see nothing," said one.

"L-look!" cried another.

As he pointed at the mesquite bushes off to one

side, his companions saw a great bear rise up there with a roar and sniff the air. The bear stood taller on his hind legs than the tallest of the young men, and he roared as fiercely as the thunder. His mouth gaped wide and red, and his teeth were bright and sharp.

"Run!" shouted one hunter. "He is coming this way!"

The tallest young man turned pale, his eyes rolled up, and he fell flat in a faint at the feet of his friends.

"Hoh, quickly! Quickly!" cried the shortest of the four still standing. "Let us take hold of him and run!"

One took his left arm, one his right. The other two took a foot apiece, and together they fled up over a hill and away. They ran and ran. Their friend sagged lower and lower between them. Still the bear came lolloping after. Each time he lost sight of the hunters, he stopped to stand up and sniff, and he gave another horrible roar.

"He will not stop until he has eaten us!" panted one as they came to the top of another hill and looked down. In the little valley below was a stream with thick groves of black walnut and pecan trees along its banks.

"Let us go down there and rest a moment in the shade," said the shortest. "The trees there will hide us."

So they went down. "He will sniff us out," said another when they came there. They set their friend down, and three sat down beside him.

The shortest stayed standing. "No," he said bravely. "I will go back and turn the bear away while you go on. But you must pay me with your rings and ear ornaments and beads, and your war paint. Then if you wait for me over the next hill, I will turn back and kill him or frighten him away."

The others gazed at him with wide eyes, but they did as he asked. They took off their rings, their beads and ear ornaments, and gave them to him. They took from their pouches the small gourd pots of paint, red and blue and yellow, that they carried for painting their faces if they needed to raid an enemy camp, and gave them to him. Then they picked up their friend and went over the next hill.

The smallest hunter turned back. Almost at once he saw the bear running toward him. So he ran toward the bear.

The bear stopped. The hunter stopped too. He opened his pouch and held up the beads and ornaments, then the paint pots, for the bear to see. "For you," he said. He returned the gifts to the pouch and set it on the ground between them. He sat down.

The bear sat down.

The hunter took out his red stone pipe, filled it, made a spark of fire, and lit it. When he made a puff of smoke, the bear stared. The hunter took another puff, then held out the pipe.

The bear sat still. Then he put out a paw, took the pipe, drew a long puff, and passed it back.

"It is good," the smallest hunter said. "Now we have peace. Now you must not chase us poor hunters. You must not behave as if we are enemies."

"Rr-mph," the bear growled. But he reached out and picked up the pouch.

So the hunter rose and went off to rejoin his friends. They were about to set off for home when the bear came over the hill behind them. The three frightened hunters leaped to their feet. They bent to lift their companion.

"No, do not run," the smallest hunter said. The others watched as the bear circled wide around them, took a drink from the creek, then circled back, and up over the hill and away.

"Hoh!" the three hunters exclaimed in admiration. "Did you see how he trembled? How he turned tail and ran?"

The fifth young man opened his eyes and lifted his head. "Has he gone?" he asked as the others helped him to his feet.

"He has," they answered, and together the five returned home to their camp. There, their tale of Big Man Who Frightens Bears made the smallest hunter famous.

No one thought to ask what became of his pouch with the ornaments and paint.

YOUNG BOY CHIEF AND HIS SISTER

Wichita

Waiksedia and his sister lived together with their dog, Little Dog. Waiksedia—whose name means "Young Boy Chief"—owned a fine bow and four handsome arrows, two painted red and two painted black. With these four arrows he had become a great hunter of deer, so he and his sister never went hungry. They always had all of the dried and fresh venison they could eat.

One morning Waiksedia's sister rose in the gray light before dawn, as she always did, left their lodge near the creek, and went with her water pot to draw water. As she dipped water from the creek into the pot, a slight movement made her look up, and she saw a deer asleep on the bank far upstream. She stood up slowly and stepped back among the trees.

"Waiksedia, my brother! Bring your bow! Come and see!" Sister called.

Waiksedia did not answer. He did not come.

"Brother! A deer! Bring your bow!"

Waiksedia did not come.

"Waiksedia! A deer! Come and see! Bring your bow!"

Waiksedia did not come until she had called four times. Then he came running, his bow in one hand, his arrows in the other. When Sister saw him slip among the willow trees along the bank, she drew back. Downstream, out of sight of the deer, she filled her pot full and turned back to their lodge.

The deer was a long way off, but that did not worry Waiksedia. He took aim and shot, and his arrow struck the deer, but as it did, it snapped in pieces and fell to the ground. He moved closer, but the deer did not turn and run, as deer do. Young Boy Chief shot another arrow, and a third and a fourth, and each one struck the deer, but fell to the ground in pieces. Then the deer raised up and looked at him.

Waiksedia stood still as a stone. He was too surprised to move. The deer was no deer, but Taahaitschidl—Big Hail Deer—the elk.

Big Hail Deer trotted toward the boy and, with a loud snort, scooped him up on its antlers. Then it turned, splashed across the stream, and galloped off.

After a while, Waiksedia's sister went down to the creek again, to discover why her brother had not returned home. All she found were the broken arrows. She gathered them up and took them back to the lodge, and she and Little Dog waited. When

Young Boy Chief had not come by midday, she went again to the creek, and followed along the bank until she came to the place where Young Boy Chief had stood. She saw the large hoofprints. "Big Hail Deer!" she cried. "*Ai!* My brother has been taken by Big Hail Deer."

At home, she told Little Dog that she was going to look for Young Boy Chief. She took her grinding stone and began to grind corn into meal for her journey. She wept as she ground, for she feared that her brother might be dead.

"Little Dog," she said, "you must stay here. I may be gone a long time, or it may be a short time, but I will bring Young Boy Chief with me. We will be hungry for meat, so you must hunt and bring plenty home for us. I will leave my gourd full of water for you when you grow thirsty."

When she had filled a deerskin sack with the cornmeal and tied a drinking gourd to her belt, she took out the magic double-ball and stick many women in those times used to travel with, and set out to find Young Boy Chief. Sometimes as she flew along she sighed and wept. Sometimes she sang, and her song was, "*Ki-di-wa-a-ta-ka-ki-da-e-da-ka. It was all my fault. It was not a deer. It was the great elk.*"

Before long she came into hill country, and saw Wokis, the mountain lion, standing atop the hill ahead.

"Stop where you are!" Wokis roared. "What are

you doing coming here? Go away. Do you hear, you ugly old sack of bones? No strangers allowed!"

But Sister was not ugly, and she was not old, and she was not bony, and so she went on. When she came to the place where the mountain lion stood, she opened her sack and poured out onto a flat stone enough ground corn for a good meal. "I am looking for my brother, Young Boy Chief," she said. "Big Hail Deer has carried him away."

"Hoh!" exclaimed Wokis. "So that was your brother! They passed a long while ago. I do not know whether Young Boy Chief was alive or dead, for Big Hail Deer is dangerous, and I keep out of his way. If you keep on through the hill country, you will find a fellow who has stronger powers than I, and he may help you. His name is Chearpeschaux."

Sister shivered, for Chearpeschaux meant "Headless Man," but she picked up her magic double-ball and stick, and sang her sad song as she traveled on.

After a time she saw a man standing on top of a hill just ahead. He held his head in the crook of his arm, and when he saw her, he shouted out, "Go back! This is my land, and I eat strangers! Go away, you filthy, scabby wart!"

But Sister was not filthy. She had no scabs. She was not a wart, and so she went on. She looked down at the ground instead of at Chearpeschaux, and kept going even when he put his head back on and ran at her with a roar louder than Wokis's. When she came up to him, she opened her sack and poured out onto a flat stone nearby enough ground corn for a good meal. "I am looking for my brother, Young Boy Chief," she said. "Big Hail Deer has carried him away."

"Hoh, you are that girl!" said Chearpeschaux. "I am sorry that I tried to frighten you. You were not wrong to come here. Soon after he carried away the brother you search for, Big Hail Deer passed by this place, but if you mean to follow them, you must be very careful. That Big Hail Deer is too fierce to fight or frighten. If you must know more, you must ask the fellow who lives in the hills past here. His name is Widadadiakisda, Bear Having Great Powers, and those powers are much stronger than mine."

So Sister went on as before with her magical double-ball and stick, weeping and singing her song, "Ki-di-wa-a-ta-ka-ki-da-e-da-ka!" until she heard an angry growl as loud as a thunderclap.

The bear who stood on the hilltop was huge, and horrible to look at. "You, girl!" he boomed. "Go away from here! Turn back or I'll smash you with boulders! No travelers, no strangers, no beak-nosed, foul-smelling, snaggletoothed women allowed on my hills!"

But Sister's nose was not a beak. She smelled

like the fresh-cut grass of her bed, of meadow flowers, and of ground corn. Her teeth were white and straight. And she was brave. She kept her head down so that she could not see the huge bear, and kept on even when a big boulder came bounding down the hill. When she was close enough to see the bear's paws, she opened her sack and poured out onto a flat rock beside the path enough ground corn for a good meal. At once Bear Having Great Powers stopped booming out, "Go away," and asked, "Are you the girl who is looking for her brother?"

"Yes, I am looking for Young Boy Chief," she said. "Big Hail Deer has carried him away."

"Then, good sister," Bear Having Great Powers said gently, "forgive my harsh words. I can tell you this: My ears are the best in the world, so I heard your brother singing all the way here after he was carried away. I do not hear him now, but I know of a fellow who can help you. His name is Old Scabby Bull. When you come to his lodge, you will see a boy-child playing outside. Take this boy up on your back and enter the lodge. Old Scabby Bull will be pleased to see you play with his favorite child and give him cornmeal. He will help you free your brother, but only if you ask again and again until he agrees."

So Sister thanked Bear Having Great Powers

and went on as before. When she came to the dugout hole in the hill that was Old Scabby Bull's lodge, she did exactly as Bear Having Great Powers had told her. Just as he said, Old Scabby Bull agreed at last to help her.

"Tomorrow we will go toward the place where Big Hail Deer lives. We will find hiding places there. It will not be easy. Before we attack Big Hail Deer, you will see your brother. If he is wounded, or starved, you must not weep. If you weep, Big Hail Deer will hear you, and both of us will die."

"I will not weep," said Young Boy Chief's sister.

The old bull made for himself a tiny bow and one arrow, and the next morning he and Sister traveled toward the place where Big Hail Deer lived. When Sister was hidden, Old Scabby Bull turned himself into a small snowbird, took up his little bow and arrow, and hid behind a tuft of grass. When at last the great elk came, the noise of a great wind came before him, and on the wind was the faint sound of Young Boy Chief singing, *"Ja-a-he-schats-as-ta-ki-di-a. . . . Na-ki-di-wa. The Elk is carrying me on his antlers. . . . I am still alive."*

As Big Hail Deer came near, he slowed a little and sniffed at the air as he passed the tuft of grass. Quickly, the snowbird hopped out and shot his arrow into the fork of the elk's nearest front hoof.

Big Hail Deer crashed to the ground.

At once, Snowbird took the string from his tiny bow and beat the elk with it, so that Big Hail Deer died. In his own shape, Old Scabby Bull lifted Young Boy Chief off the beast's antlers and carried him to his sister, who, with Big Hail Deer safely dead, could weep to see how thin her brother was, and how scarred with antler wounds. Together she and Old Scabby Bull went to the creek near the old bull's home and led the sick young chief to the water. He plunged in, and Old Scabby Bull called to him four times, saying, "Waiksedia, come out of the water. Your sister has come a long way for you."

When Young Boy Chief stepped out of the water, all of his hurts were healed, and he held in one hand his bow and in the other his four beautiful arrows.

He and Sister stayed with Old Scabby Bull's people long enough for Young Boy Chief to go hunting. To thank the old bull for his kindness, Young Boy Chief brought back to his camp enough meat to feed his people for many days. Then he and Sister started for home. Sister used her magic double-ball and stick as before, and Young Boy Chief used the magic in his arrows to travel with.

When at last they came to their lodge, they saw that weeds had grown up all around. No Little Dog ran out to greet them at the doorway of the lodge.

When they looked inside, they discovered that he had starved to death, for all they saw was a heap of hair and bones. He had been so lonely that he had eaten no meat and drunk no water. Sister quickly gathered up the hair and bones, went down to the creek, and threw them into the water. Then she stood on the bank and called four times, "Little Dog, come out of the water! I have brought our brother home!" At her fourth call, Little Dog leaped out of the water and ran to greet Young Boy Chief and Sister.

For a time they lived together as they had before, but though Young Boy Chief hunted as before, and though they had all the meat they needed, Young Boy Chief was not happy. He told Sister that because of the trouble and hurts he had suffered and the hard journey she had had to save him, every day he feared that some other terrible thing would happen. He wished to be safe above the dangers of the world. So first they found a good home for Little Dog. Then they built a fire out under the sky, took a gourd full of water, and poured it onto the flames.

As the smoke and steam rose up into the sky, they rose up too—and became eagles, far above the dangers of the world.

ABOUT THE STORYTELLERS

The short notes below will tell you a little of the history of the peoples who once told the tales in *Hold Up the Sky*. Readers of—and listeners to—the tales can learn much more about the history and way of life of the storytellers' people on the Internet. Not all of the Indian nations have Web sites, but both *www.texasindians.com* and the "Handbook of Texas Online" site have alphabetical entries for many of the nations, bands, and tribes. If you like to browse the Web and do not find an entry for "Caddo tribe," for example, try "Caddo Indians" or "Caddo Nation." You would find that the tribe's official Web site is at *www.caddonation.com*. The "Handbook of Texas Online" can be found at *www.tsha.utexas.edu/handbook/online*.

THE CADDO NATION

The name Caddo is a short form of Kadohadacho, which means "the real chiefs." The Caddo peoples of Texas included the Eyeish and the tribes of the Hasinai and Kadohadacho Confederacies. The term Caddoan also refers to the language family to which they and the Pawnee, Arikara, and Wichita tribes belong. It was also once the name of a separate tribe within the Kadohadacho Confederacy. To avoid confusion, they usually are referred to as the

Caddo Proper. It can be difficult to be sure whether a tale identified as Caddo, such as "Coyote and the Seven Brothers" or "How Rabbit Stole Mountain Lion's Teeth," was told by a Caddo Proper story-teller or a member of some other tribe of the Caddo Nation.

The Caddo were farmers and traders. The Spanish conquerors in the seventeenth century, and the French in the eighteenth, described them as intelligent, friendly, industrious, brave, and true to their word. After the United States bought the Louisiana Territory, the Louisiana Caddo joined the Caddo in Texas in 1835, but by 1859 hostile white settlers had forced them north out of Texas and into the Oklahoma Indian Territory. Their descendants live in Oklahoma still.

COMANCHE

The Comanche people called themselves the Nerm or Numunuh, "the people of people." Originally a branch of the Northern Shoshone, they acquired horses toward the end of the seventeenth century and ventured south out of the Rocky Mountains and onto the plains. The success of these buffalo-hunting expeditions, the better climate, and opportunities for trade encouraged the entire nation to migrate. Soon much of Texas was Comanche country, and the bands followed the buffalo herds as nomads. They were hospitable and generous, great horsemen, hunters, and raiders, and were formidable foes to the Caddo, Plains Apache, and Kiowa.

The French first encountered Comanches in 1724, and in 1746 negotiated peace between them and the Caddo. The Comanche made peace with the Kiowa in 1790 but did not sign a treaty with the United States until 1834. In 1854 Texas tried to exile them to a reservation, but the Comanche remained hostile to the invading settlers. They continued raiding and were often at war, for the Texan and U.S. governments broke one treaty after another. Not until 1875 were the Comanche forced to surrender. Reservation life and the passing of the buffalo meant that their old Plains way of life was at an end. Many today still live in the Comanche Federal Trust Area in southwestern Oklahoma.

KADOHADACHO

The Kadohadacho, who lived on the north side of the Red River, where Texas, Arkansas, and Louisiana meet, were the leaders of the group of allies known as the Kadohadacho Confederacy. Their allies—the Cahinnio, Nanatsoho, Upper Nasoni, Upper Natchitoches, and Upper Yatasi—lived along the south side of the Red River and near the Ouachita River in southern Arkansas. The first

Europeans to meet the Kadohadacho were the survivors of a French expedition in 1687, and in 1719 the French established a trading post near them. Over the next hundred years the Kadohadacho suffered many losses from attacks by the warlike Osage and twice moved farther downriver into Louisiana. In 1824 they and the Quapaw signed a treaty with the U.S., agreeing to return to the old Caddo country along the upper Red River. In 1835, as a result of a new treaty, the Kadohadacho agreed to cross the border into Texas, leaving the U.S. In Texas they settled near their fellow Caddoans, the Hasinai. There the white settlers, angered by Comanche and Apache raids, turned on the friendly Kadohadacho and their kindred, too. The Caddoan tribes became a more united people during these troubles, and from that time all began to be called simply Caddo. In 1859 they left Texas for a new reservation in southwestern Oklahoma, and many of their descendants live there still.

KIOWA

In their own Kiowa language the name Kiowa means "principal people." Their tradition tells that long ago they lived in the mountains at the head of the Missouri River in Montana. In the early nineteenth century they moved down into the Great Plains. There they learned how to ride horses and hunt buffalo, but the Cheyenne and Arapaho gradually forced them southward. In 1840 the Kiowa at last made peace with them, and that peace was never broken.

On the Southern Plains the Kiowa found that the country south of the Arkansas River was claimed by the Comanche. After a time they, too, became allies, and together the two peoples made raids into Mexico. The Kiowa themselves became bitter enemies of the invading Americans, and in 1868 they were moved with the Comanche and Kiowa-Apache to a reservation in Oklahoma. Their present-day tribal headquarters is in Anadarko, Oklahoma.

KIOWA-APACHE

The people of this small tribe were called Tagui by the Kiowa, and Gata'ka by the Pawnee and the French. Their myths and oral traditions tell of a northern origin, like the Kiowa, and they seem to have joined with the Kiowa for their own protection. They came to be called Kiowa-Apache because they were allied to and lived alongside the Kiowa, and because their language—which they kept—belongs to the same language family, the Athapascan, as that of the Apache. Except for the two years from 1865 to 1867, their history has been much the same as that of the Kiowa. At that time they separated from the

Kiowa and were joined to the southern Cheyenne and Arapaho because they did not share the Kiowan hostility toward the whites.

KITKEHAHKI, SOUTH BAND PAWNEE

The Pawnee, another of the Caddoan peoples, migrated north from the Caddoan homelands near the Red River to what is now southern Nebraska and northern Oklahoma. The Kitkehahki, Pitahauerats, and Chaui bands of the Pawnee remained in the upper Southern Plains when the larger Skidi band moved farther north. They had few contacts with the Spanish and French until later than Native American peoples living farther south, but in the eighteenth century they traded with the French and became their allies. They were farmers but also became superb horsemen who lived the traditional nomadic life of the plains on their summer and winter buffalo hunts.

In the nineteenth century—in 1818—they signed their first treaty with the United States, and despite troubles with the settlers and the government, they never made war against the United States. Many served as scouts with the army in the 1860s and 1870s. In the 1870s they ceded to the government what was left of their Nebraska lands and moved to federal Oklahoma Indian Territory.

KITSAI

The name Kitsai—or Kitchai, the name they called themselves—means "going in wet sand." Their Caddoan language was halfway between that of the Pawnee and the Wichita, and the Pawnee translated *Kitsai* as "water turtle." By the beginning of the eighteenth century they had arrived in northern Texas, where they stayed until assigned with other small tribes in 1855 to a small reservation on the Brazos River. Only three years later, threatened with being wiped out by the white settlers, they had to flee to safety with the Wichita people in Oklahoma. They remained with them, but by 1910 their numbers had dwindled sadly from what had been about five hundred in 1690 to only ten.

LIPAN APACHE

Several related tribes that spoke Athapascan languages were called Apache, and of these the Lipan in the eighteenth and early nineteenth centuries ranged from eastern New Mexico across western Texas, and south as far as the Gulf of Mexico. Between 1757 and 1767 the Spanish built three missions for them, but these, one after another, were destroyed by their Comanche and Wichita enemies. After siding with the Texans against the Comanche in 1839, the Lipan themselves were persecuted by the settlers and in 1856 were pushed into Mexico. There they remained until, in 1905, the last nineteen Lipan were brought across the border to the Mescalero Apache reservation in New Mexico. Their descendants still live in New Mexico.

OSAGE (WAZHAZHE)

The European-American name Osage for these people came about because the early French explorers heard and wrote down the name *Wazhazhe,* as it would be spelled in French. Like the Quapaw, Omaha, Ponca, and Kaw peoples, who belonged to the same Southern Siouan family of languages, the Osage traditions are those of the ancient Mississippian culture that was centered in the Ohio and Mississippi valley regions. Their homeland in the Southern Plains ranged from the southern parts of Missouri and Kansas down into Oklahoma and Arkansas. As farmers, the Osage settled in villages and grew corn and other crops, but also set up camps on the plains for hunting buffalo.

Because they lived between the European settlements and the tribes farther west, the Osage not only could control trade between them, but, earlier than other tribes, had the guns to defend their lands from raiders. Their neighbors found them fierce and warlike, but though enemy tribes could not defeat them, treaties signed with the United States between 1809 and 1870 did. The Osage lost more than one hundred million acres of land. In 1872 they had the good fortune to buy a part of their old hunting country in Oklahoma from the Cherokee, where rich deposits of oil and gas were discovered in the 1890s.

Tawakoni

The Tawakoni were one of the bands of the Wichita peoples. Their name was said to mean either "a river bend among red hills" or "neck of land in the water." They were closely related to the Wichita band, whose language was very like their own. French explorers met the Tawakoni in 1719 in central Oklahoma, but later the Tawakoni and other bands of the Wichita peoples were pushed southward to the Red River and northern Texas. They defeated a strong attack by the Spanish in 1759, but by 1781 they had moved on south and west to the Brazos River. They were a party to treaties with Texas and then the United States in the mid-nineteenth century but were moved to a reservation on the Brazos in 1855. Like so many other peoples, they were forced out of Texas by hostile white settlers and in 1859 were officially joined with the Wichita on an Oklahoma reservation. According to the U.S. census of 1910, only one Tawakoni survived.

TEJAS (HASINAI)

The Spanish mistook the word *Tejas,* or "Texas," for the name of the Caddoan Hasinai, when it was really the greeting of "friend" or "our own people" that was used among the Hasinai tribes. The Hasinai confederacy of eight tribes included the Anadarko, Hainai, Nabedache, Nacanish, Nacogdoche, Namidish, Nasoni, and Neches. The tale "The Beginning of the World" is thought to be from the Hainai. Theirs was the chief village of the confederacy, and their priest-chief had authority over the other chiefs, or *caddis.*

The Hasinai lived in northeast Texas between the upper Trinity and Neches Rivers. They got along well with the Spanish and French colonists, who were more interested in trade than land. They suffered, though—as did many Native American tribes—from being introduced to new diseases and strong alcoholic drink, from the loss of their own culture, and from the growing pressure from white and Indian settlers. Early in the nineteenth century they were joined by the Louisiana Caddo, and after the Cherokee War in 1839 they were forced to migrate west. In 1855 they were placed on a reservation but four years later fled into the federal Oklahoma Indian Territory when the settlers threatened to massacre them.

TONKAWA

The Tonkawa were at first a group of related but independent bands who were enemies of the Hasinai to the east, the Apache to the west, and other neighbors. Tonkawa, the neighboring Waco people's name for them, means "they all stay together." Later, as the name suggests, they came together into a single tribe under a head chief. When in the eighteenth century the Spanish settled them in missions, they suffered from terrible epidemics, Apache raids, and the alien way of life. After the Spanish gave up the missions, the Tonkawa remained in central Texas and were the settlers' enemies. In the nineteenth century they made peace with and became allies of the Apache, and were allies, too, of the Texans and the United States. Even so, in 1855 they and several other tribes were sent to a reservation on the Brazos River. Attacked there by the settlers, the Tonkawa were then moved into Oklahoma, but in 1862 a force of Caddo, Shawnee, and other old foes descended on their camp there. Almost half of the three hundred Tonkawa were killed, and the survivors had nowhere to go but back into Texas. There, some years later, they were settled at Fort Griffin. In the 1880s the last remnant and a few Lipan Apaches were given a small reservation in Oklahoma. The number of Tonkawa had dwindled to fifty-one by

1937. By 1951, because of intermarriage with other peoples and with whites, they had ceased to be a separate tribe.

Waco

The Waco were a small band of the Wichita people, and some believe that their original homeland was in Oklahoma. In Texas they lived in two villages, a large one on the Brazos River, where the city of Waco now stands, and a smaller one at Hueco (Waco) Springs on the Guadalupe River. Farmers for most of the year, like many groups in northern Texas they left their villages in winter to follow the buffalo on the Southern Plains, living in tipis in their hunting camps along the way.

In 1859, 171 Waco were reported living in Texas. Soon afterward they were removed from Texas to Oklahoma and joined with the Tawakoni and Wichita bands. By 1910 the U.S. census listed only five surviving Waco.

Wichita

The Wichita peoples included the Wichita, Tawakoni, Waco, Tawehash, and Yscani bands. Their name of Wichita came from the word *wits*, meaning "man," but they referred to themselves as *Kitikiti'sh*— "raccoon eyes"—because the tattooed patterns around their eyes looked rather like a raccoon's mask.

A number of the names for them in their neighbors' languages meant "tattooed people."

The Spanish explorer Francisco Vásquez de Coronado met the Wichita band near the Arkansas River in central Kansas in 1541 and wrote that there were twenty-five Wichita towns. However, over time enemy tribes from the east and north pushed them farther and farther south. In 1719 a French trader found them and several of the other bands in Oklahoma, and by 1772 they were near the Oklahoma-Texas border along the upper Red River and in Texas on the upper Brazos. They remained in the region, but in 1858 a U.S. Army unit pursuing Comanches destroyed their village at Rush Spring, so in the following year the Wichita survivors joined up with the remaining Waco and other bands. During the Civil War they took refuge in Kansas, and on their return in 1867 they were settled on a reservation near present-day Anadarko, Oklahoma. The Wichita tribal headquarters is still in Anadarko.

ABOUT THE STORIES

The tales I have retold in *Hold Up the Sky* have been told to generation after generation of Native American audiences by the storytellers of their tribes. For all we know, some could have their roots in tales a thousand years old. It is sad to think that more stories were lost than saved as the early, and then later, peoples of Texas and the Southern Plains dwindled, mingled with other tribes, or were destroyed by disease, war, or the hostility of white settlers. Native American storytellers still told the tales they heard from their elders, but missionaries and the schools for Native American children hoped to erase this traditional lore and make the children into "good little whites." Not until the latter part of the nineteenth century did travelers and scholars begin to listen, and to value and to write down the tales they heard.

It is in the printed records that these men and women published that I found the tales I have retold. Stories always change a little from teller to teller. Some tales in time were influenced by those of allied tribes, or of European stories. Those in *Hold Up the Sky* are also different in that, though the content of the stories is unchanged, they are told in my own words. The tales that were my sources can be found in the books that follow.

Elliott Canonge, in *Comanche Texts* (1958), pages 21-23, gives a translation of "The Great Meatball" from the Comanche language.

George A. Dorsey, in *The Mythology of the Wichita* (Carnegie Institution of Washington, Publication no. 21, 1904), records on page 289 the Tawakoni story "Coyote and the Smallest Snake," told to him by a man named Ignorant Woman! The Waco tale "The Thunderbird Woman" appears on pages 120-23, and the Wichita tale "Young Boy Chief and His Sister" on pages 218-24.

In *Traditions of the Caddo* (1905), Mr. Dorsey has recorded "How Rabbit Stole Mountain Lion's Teeth" (on pages 85-86) and two versions of "Slaying the Monsters," told by Wing and White Bread (on pages 47-50). In *Traditions of the Osage* (in the *Field Columbian Museum Anthropological Series*, vol. 7) he recorded "Mountain Lion and the Four Sisters" (pages 18-19) and "The Boy Who Killed the Hill" (page 42).

On pages 59-61 in "Coyote and the Six Brothers," he records the story of an old woman's youngest son and his six brothers, which I retell as "Coyote and the Seven Brothers." In his article "Wichita Tales" in *The Journal of American Folklore,* vol. 15, (1902), Mr. Dorsey includes on pages 223-28 the tale I tell as "The Monsters and the Flood" as one part of a longer story.

Mattie Austin Hatcher translates the story I call "The Beginning of the World" as part of a longer story in "Myths of the Tejas Indians" (*Texas and Southwestern Lore,* one of the publications of the Texas Folk-Lore Society Series, vol. 6 (1927), pages 109-10.) Her sources were the writings of early Spanish missionaries Fray Jesús María de Casañas (*Informe,* 1691) and Fray Isidro Espinosa (*Chronica,* c. 1720).

Harry Hoijer gives translations of "Coyote and Mouse" (on page 41), and "The Tonkawa and the Bear" (on page 79) in *Tonkawa Texts,* volume 72 of the *University of California Publications in Linguistics* Series (1972).

Alexander Lesser's "Kitsai Texts" translates "Coyote Frees the Buffalo" (pages 45-49), which was told to him by Kai Kai, a woman in her eighties. The article appears in *Caddoan Texts* (vol. 2, no. 1 of the *International Journal of American Linguistics, Native American Texts Series,* 1977), edited by

Douglas R. Parks. In the same volume Mr. Parks, in "Pawnee Texts: Skiri and South Band," presents the southern Pawnee tale "Coyote and Possum" (on pages 75-79).

*Alice Marriott and Carol K. Rachlin, in *American Indian Mythology* (1968), reprint on pages 128-30 the Comanche tale "Why the Bear Waddles When He Walks." This book is still in print, and may be available in your public library or bookstore.

Among the stories recorded in J. Gilbert McAllister's article "Kiowa-Apache Tales" are "How Coyote Made the Sun" (pages 22-25); "How the Poor Boy Won His Wife" (pages 82-85), told by Solomon Katchin; and "The Ghost Woman" (pages 93-97), narrated by Big Lobo Wolf. The article can be found in *The Sky Is My Tipi,* edited by Mody C. Boatright. It is volume 22 of the *Publications of the Texas Folklore Society* series (1949).

Morris Edward Opler's *Myths and Legends of the Lipan Apache Indians,* volume 36 in the *Memoirs of the American Folklore Society* series (1940), was the source for my retellings of "The Quarrel

Between Wind and Thunder" (page 86), "Coyote Helps Lizard Hold Up the Sky" (page 150), "Coyote Flies with the Geese" (pages 108-9), and "The Fight Between the Animals and the Insects" (pages 199–200).

Elsie Clews Parsons's *Kiowa Tales* (*Memoirs of the American Folklore Society,* vol. 22, 1929) was the source for my retellings of "Sendeh Sings to the Prairie Dogs" (pages 27-29), told by Kumole, a.k.a. Big Hand; and "White Fox" (pages 69-70), told by Kiabo ("Rescued").

H. H. St. Clair II collected and R. H. Lowie edited the original version of "The Deserted Children," which can be found on pages 275-76 of "Shoshone and Comanche Tales," in *The Journal of American Folklore,* volume 22 (1909).

ABOUT THE AUTHOR

Jane Louise Curry, storyteller and author of more than thirty books for young people, was born in Ohio and grew up there and in Pennsylvania. She studied at Indiana University of Pennsylvania, UCLA, Stanford, and the University of London. Ms. Curry taught writing and children's literature at Stanford before turning to writing full-time. She lives in Los Angeles and spends a part of each year in London.